FLIGHT OF
THE SWAN

Lacey Dancer

A KISMET™ Romance

METEOR PUBLISHING CORPORATION
Bensalem, Pennsylvania

To David. When you weave the image of
a hero, it's nice to have a prototype.
You're mine.

LACEY DANCER

Lacey Dancer is a woman of many interests. Her
husband and writing are numbers one and two; but
that doesn't stop her from collecting antique saltcel-
lars, an assortment of farm animals, and learning
organic gardening. Roses and peonies are her favorite
flowers and weaving words into dreams of love the
best way to earn a living.

Other books by Lacey Dancer:

PROLOGUE

Dawn spread across the Florida sky, a pink blush of innocence for the beginning of a new day, gold for the opportunities all life would have of the coming moments, silver for the purity of principles, gray for the masses that would not see beyond their small empty worlds, blue for the valor of the brave, and white for the virgin hours that had yet to know the touch of a man.

Martin Richland, III, got out of his car, his eyes on the sunrise unfurling its cloak of glory for his gaze alone. He traced the fingers of light across the heavens, allowing the poetic, idealistic side of his nature free rein over the silent extravaganza of color. These days, in the normal course of events, no part of the softer side of his personality was ever allowed to surface. The past had taught him the value of keeping the soft core of his thoughts, the gentle touch of his ideas, hidden, protected. Now, only in these moments of solitude, did he permit himself to feel deeply, strongly. To the rest of the world, he turned a cynical eye, an unshockable mien, and nerves so cool that any problem, no matter how difficult, slipped right past his emotions to lodge in the analytical section of his mind. Despite the beauty of the dawn, he smiled grimly to himself, thinking of what his new friends would say if they could see him in his worn clothes trotting over the school's track, working up an honest sweat in the public grounds when his wealth and position entitled him to any number of exclusive club memberships. They would simply shake their heads over his latest eccentricity and keep their questions to themselves. Rich, as he was known to his intimates, had no rules but his own, no needs but those he chose, and no wants that he couldn't buy. Because he hated idleness he worked, for Luck Enterprises to be specific. His official job title was vice president, holding thirty percent of the stock. In truth, his association with the dynamic Joshua Luck was more complex, more demanding, and far less definable than a single office could cover. Which was why he needed the physical exertion that he sought each morning, rain or sun.

Stretching his long body in a sinuous move that made every muscle ripple smoothly beneath golden skin, he glanced idly around the deserted high school. A sudden rip of water caught his ears almost the second his eyes focused on the pool with its high diving platform. Startled, vaguely annoyed to find his solitude invaded, he moved to the shadow of the tree beneath which he had parked. The last thing he wanted was to discover someone else in what he had begun to think of as his private space. He watched the slender arms of the swimmer cut gracefully through the water to the edge of the pool.

His breath dammed in his throat as the most exquisitely curved woman seemed to rise out of the blue-green depths as though defying gravity. The body was pure male fantasy. From the long legs superbly displayed in a black French-cut suit to the gently flaring hips tucking into a two-hand-span waist and then lifting to soft swells so beautifully modeled that Rodin couldn't have done a better job of sculpting her figure. Dark hair hung in a long plait down a slender back, the ends brushing gently against the full swell of her bottom as she walked.

"Where did you come from?" he whispered, not even realizing his thoughts had been spoken to the breeze that caressed her bare skin. The rising sun seemed to love the pearl-and-ivory flesh, gilding her limbs, light playing tag with her body with each movement.

Desire, swift, unexpected, and fiery, swept through him, stunning him with the sensation that had, of late, become more of a conditioned response commanded by his partners than an honest expression of wanting. His tawny eyes narrowed, his muscles tightening against the demand for control his mind placed on its reaction. He tried to look away, tried to move away, but her swaying walk, the glide of muscle over bone that carried her to the ladder and the climb aloft held him fascinated. There was no wasted motion in this woman, no attempt to seduce, no goal to titillate the senses. Her grace was real, her figure a dream, and her poise as she walked to the end of the board complete. As she pushed out into a reverse swan, he followed her dive, marveling at the line, the power, and the delicacy of her skill. Again there was that rip of water that said the entry was as near perfect as humanly possible. Once again, she stroked through the water, coming out of the pool in almost the exact spot as before and with that same distinctive lift and twist. As he watched, the woman took the long, old-fashioned plait of water-darkened hair hanging down her back and brought it over her shoulder to wring out the excess moisture. Beads of sweat formed on his forehead with every unconsciously seductive movement. The tails of the braid teased at her right breast, drawing images of silken sheets and her nude beneath him. He inhaled deeply, stunned at the sharp need to announce himself. He was no peeping male and yet he couldn't seem to move from the shadows into the light.

Christiana Drake stared around the empty school-yard, trying to pinpoint the source of her uneasiness. It hadn't been present when she had arrived at the school nor during her first dive. But it was definitely here now. A presence, intense, unwavering. She should have felt threatened, for she could see no one, only a car parked far away from her own which she must have missed when she arrived. Her gaze skimmed over the empty area, lingering on the few shadows cast by the trees dotted about the parking area. Again and again her eyes went back to the largest shadow, which shaded the racy sports car. No movement disturbed the silence and yet she couldn't look away from that tree. Every instinct said a man stood beneath those branches. Her hands stilled as she stared across the space. No matter how hard she looked she could spot no trace of movement, but she knew he was there, watching.

Walking slowly to the lounge where she had laid her clothes and towel she tried to understand why her first inclination wasn't to leave. After all, she had avoided audiences for years. She hated being on display in any way. Had it been any other morning but this one, she would have left. But she needed to be in the water. She needed the freedom of flight and the concentration of striving for the perfect dive. She looked back to the tree, coming to a decision. Let him watch. Flipping her braid back over her shoulder, she strode briskly to the ladder. After all, she would see him before he approached her if that were his aim. And she was certainly equipped with enough defenses that she was as safe as anyone could be on the streets these days. She walked to the end of the board, her mind automatically concentrating on the job at hand.

Her muscles flexed, balance a perfect rhythm in her movements. She pushed up and off, her length an arrow aimed to the heavens, then a twisting storm rushing to the water below. Grace, then power. Beauty, then courage. The water received her gently, tearing for the thrust of her body into its warmth.

Rich leaned against the tree, his eyes never leaving the woman. He knew that she sensed his presence. There had been a challenge in that walk, an I-don't-give-a-damn-if-you-look toss to her head as she had mounted the ladder. A smile tugged at his lips, humor at her and himself softening the edges of need as he settled into being an audience of one. He couldn't see her features clearly enough to read her expression but he knew he'd never forget her body or her skill. And for now they seemed enough. He had been disappointed so many times in the past that just this once he wanted this illusion to stay intact.

Christiana slipped out of her damp suit, thinking about her practice. One full hour of diving and not once had she felt her audience's attention wane. She had known his eyes followed her every move and still she had mounted the platform for jump after jump. In fact, she had found that she had worked even harder to reach the ultimate in perfection with every leap. She frowned as she walked into the mirrored bathroom, her figure reflected upon itself. Stopping, she stared at her body, the well-endowed proportions that had caused her too many problems to forget and too few solutions to remember. Men responded to her measurements, never to the woman. Greedy male groping, fighting curious hands even after all the years of fending off such behavior had left its mark on her heart if not her flesh. She had learned the value of concealing clothing and a clear-eyed look. And along the way she had learned a number of interesting moves guaranteed to get her out of tight corners. She smiled faintly at her memories. Once she had been so uptight about her physical appearance. But somehow turning thirty had settled her thinking. She had come to accept her lot in life, taking pleasure in her career and finding amusement in the masculine interest that inevitably came her way. She still didn't like the attention she received but she had finally found a sense of humor about the situation.

She peered at her reflection deciding there were positives. Her years sat lightly on her shoulders. Few lines marred her face and no gray sprinkled her soft brown hair with highlights. Her diving kept her body at peak physical condition and the demands of her work in Europe had kept her mind constantly challenged by the cosmopolitan atmosphere and the multitude of cultures with which she had come in contact. All things considered, she had a good life, with no one to answer to but herself and a range of choices that few could rival.

Turning from her reflection, Christiana stepped into the shower. But now it was time to come home to the land of her birth. Her accent was more English than American, her thinking more a spectrum of belief systems rather than one, and her future had coalesced into a need for a permanent base. As the water sluiced over her curves, she considered tomorrow and all the days that would follow. She wasn't even sure she could turn her back on her training and all that she had become to settle in one place, but she knew she wanted to try. As she left the shower stall to dry herself, the phone rang. Wrapping a towel around her dripping body, she padded into the bedroom to answer.

"Marie, what are you doing at the office this early? I looked for you when I got back, but you had gone. Anything wrong?" Christiana asked in surprise on hearing her temporary hostess's voice.

"That depends on your answer to my next question," Marie said, grimacing. "I know you're tired and I know you told me you wanted to take a month off before you went on our job rolls, but I need your help."

Christiana sat down on the twin bed, her brow wrinkling in a concerned frown. Marie sounded desperate. "You know I'd do almost anything for you. Besides, I owe you one for letting me room with you until I find my own place. What do you need? A substitute?"

"I wish it were that simple." Marie sighed deeply then took the plunge. "I have a full-time, live-in situation for you."

Christiana's immediate reaction was to refuse. Apart from being exhausted from almost forty-eight hours of transatlantic flying, she wasn't sure she wanted a live-in position of any kind. But Marie and she had been friends through life's various trials, the kind of friends that needed no close personal contact to cement and maintain their tie. "Drop the other shoe," she murmured.

Marie sighed again, only this time with relief. "I know I'm asking a lot, but this is a big break for my 'baby.' "

Christiana smiled faintly at the nickname Marie had given her new domestic employment agency. "Stop stalling and get on with it. My curiosity is killing me."

"All right. One of Jacksonville's most influential

and charismatic couples is in dire need of a nanny for their twins. The children are four years old, one boy and one girl. The house is spectacular, set on the St. John's. The salary is twice the going rate and the position is an immediate fill. You'll have your own quarters, a private line, and a car for your exclusive use. Two days off a week and the nights can be arranged as well.''

"Dream posts rarely come gift-wrapped. What's the catch?'' Christiana asked, knowing from ten years in the baby-minding business to beware of parents with gold-plated promises. "I suppose the children are monsters and the husband is a believer in the upstairs maid philosophy.''

"None of the above. You know I wouldn't do that to you," Marie was quick to reassure her.

"I'm sorry," Christiana murmured, rubbing her temple lightly. "Put my reaction down to tiredness."

"The Lucks are special. I think you'll like them very much, and I can't think of anyone who wouldn't give their best mink to have you handling their children."

"Flattery. You *are* desperate."

Marie ignored the comment to continue, "I've met both of the Lucks. She's a writer, probably wrote those books on sexuality and eccentricity. He's dynamic and definitely interested in no other woman on this planet but his wife. They have a full social and professional life, but there seem to be problems coming out of the blending of two really caring parents with a multitude of demands which get in the way of the time they want to spend with their children. Plus, it seems that Josh and his friends are masculine dynamite to a number of feminine fuses,

namely the other eight nannies that are your predecessors. Knowing how you feel about track shoes
and octopus hands, I thought this setup might just
appeal to you. And it is a straightforward situation.
You won't be required to act as a bodyguard for the
children. There is an extensive in-house security
team and the grounds are protected by a high fence
and dogs.''

Mentally shrugging her shoulders, Christiana agreed,
''All right. I'll talk to Mrs. Luck. But I won't promise anything.''

''I'm not worried. When you meet Pippa I think
you'll find that you won't have any trouble deciding
to accept a place in their home.'' Marie flipped
through her rolodex. ''I'll call her now and set up
the appointment. Then call you back.''

''Might as well make it this morning,'' she suggested, glancing to her half-unpacked suitcases. ''At
least I won't have to do much if I do decide to take
it.''

''*I* owe *you* one,'' Marie replied before hanging
up.

''All right, you little monsters. I'm getting you a
new nanny today, so try to be on your best behavior
for just this once. Your daddy is about ready to enlist
in the Foreign Legion and take me with him.'' Pippa
gazed down at her children, receiving two wicked
grins in response. Who would have ever thought life
for her could hold so much joy and love. Or so much
chaos, she thought with a mental sigh.

''Okay, Mama,'' Lori agreed, casting a quick look
at her brother.

"We'll be good," Joshua Jr., added, looking so angelic that Pippa decided something was up.

Pippa studied the pair, knowing it was useless to try to pry their plans out of them. When they were born she was positive the devil had rubbed his hands with glee as he emptied his bag of tricks into each fertile brain. What one couldn't think up, the other certainly could. "You are treading on thin ice, you two," she said sternly, despite the laughter gleaming in her pale eyes.

Lori got to her feet, jamming her hand in the pocket of her pink jeans. "We got you a present this morning, Mama," she said softly, lifting a closed fist invitingly.

Distracted, Pippa glanced at her daughter, charmed by the gesture and the little girl's smile. She went down on her knees and held out her hand.

"You have to close your eyes," J. Jr. commanded, getting into the act.

Pippa closed her lashes, then opened them quickly, suddenly remembering the last time she had one of their presents. "This isn't a snake, is it?" she demanded suspiciously.

Two heads shook as one. "You'll like this. We promise."

She studied both faces, faintly reassured by the way they stared back at her. Whatever it was couldn't be too terrible if they could look so innocent. "All right. But I warn you if this isn't nice, I'm going to scream so loud neither one of you will be able to hear for a month."

Christiana drove to the Lucks, highly curious about the household that might be her home for months, possibly years, to come. Marie had told her just enough to whet her appetite, a smooth move she decided as she turned into a curving drive manned by a guard at the gate. As she eased up the hill she noticed a pair of sleek Dobermans quartering the grounds. The security measures were extensive, but if the facts about Joshua Luck's company that Marie had given her on the second call were even half correct, she could see why such measures were necessary. There was a wrought-iron fence around the house creating a yard within the compound of emerald lawn that stretched to the river. It was a beautiful home, lovingly tended and, again according to Marie, one of the largest and most luxurious in the area. She got out of the car and took a moment to look over the view. It was incredibly panoramic with Jacksonville rising out of its concrete and steel skirts across the river. The bridges connecting the two pieces of land were elongated spiderwebs, and the ships churning up the water, small toys to delight a child. Smiling at her own whimsy, she rang the bell. A second later the door opened to the most dour face she had ever seen. This had to be the housekeeper Elsa, whom Marie had warned her about. At that moment a muted scream sounded from the second floor.

Reflexes trained over a decade of crisis-handling took over. Without thinking, Christiana shouldered passed the housekeeper and raced up the stairs. A short oath, chopped off, gave her the direction once she reached the hall at the top of the steps. She shot through the open door, stopping short on seeing a slender woman kneeling on the area rug, faced by two wide-eyed children. The woman held a fat, mottled-green-and-gray frog as though it were a powder puff as she glared at her offspring.

"Without a doubt, I should have gotten you two a jailer," Pippa announced firmly, her pale eyes flashing.

Knowing how vulnerable children could be, Christiana was always one to take up for the young. She stepped forward, intending to intervene. Before she got the chance, the woman grabbed the little boy, laughing as he squealed for mercy when she tucked the frog into his T-shirt.

"So you want to play yucky games, do you?" Pippa caught her daughter before she could scoot away. "Going somewhere, my pretty," Pippa added in her best Simon Legree leer.

Lori giggled, twisting and turning to escape as her brother tried to fish the toad out of his clothes.

Elsa, panting from her run, planted her hands on her hips and glowered at the trio. "I brought the nanny up. But I could have saved myself the trouble. She'll be wanting to leave now that she has seen what these two limbs of Satan and their mother can do."

Pippa glanced over her shoulder, staring up, up, and up into eyes so peaceful and clear that she did a mental double-take. The face was not beautiful in the conventional sense, and yet there was something compelling about Christiana Drake. Pippa studied her, taking her time, letting her writer's eye catalogue the woman. Her body was hidden under layers of concealing clothing, but Pippa would have bet her last book on the curves beneath being worth a second look. Her hands were too elegantly formed and her ankles too slim for her figure to be what the clothes proclaimed. Once again she stared into Christiana's eyes, impressed and curious by the younger woman's self-possession. Not since meeting Josh's brother Joe had she seen a person with such inner control and contentment. She rose without breaking eye contact and held out her hand, her instinct telling her that Christiana was the person she wanted to care for her children.

"I'm Pippa Luck and these are the diabolical duo, J. Jr. and Lori. Tell me we haven't sent you running for the hills and you're hired."

Christiana was fully aware she was being weighed and tested. Her lips tipped up as she looked over the silver-haired, pale-eyed trio. She had no idea what Joshua Luck looked like, but his children had definitely inherited their mother's coloring and, if the glint in three pairs of eyes was any indication, the same turn of mind.

"I never was good at refusing a challenge," she murmured, accepting the gesture with a laugh. She glanced at the frog J. Jr. held, then at the mischievous little boy himself. "And frogs are my best friends. Snakes, too. And mice."

Pippa shuddered. "The last you can leave out unless you've got a case of smelling salts handy."

Christiana returned her attention to her prospective employer, deciding that she could easily like this woman very much. Her manner was easy, her beauty, though blindingly apparent, sat so simply on its owner's shoulders that one tended to forget the looks for the personality and life that shone out of the light-blue eyes. Her clothes were skimpy to say the least, but there didn't seem to be an ounce of woman-to-woman competitor in her behavior. If

Pippa Luck had ever been jealous or vindictive toward another, Christiana would have eaten her best swimsuit.

"Elsa, would you ask your niece to come up for a little while?" Pippa asked, turning to the house-keeper, who still hovered in the doorway.

Elsa grunted before stomping off.

Pippa laughed. "She isn't that bad," she said to Christiana. "She just hasn't gotten over having me here and I doubt she'll ever recover from my set of bookends."

"We are not bookends, Mommy," Lori piped up. "And Elsa likes us lots. She makes cookies with faces, but she says not to tell you or Daddy. Says Daddy would eat 'em all up if you didn't."

Pippa chuckled in delight as a young girl rushed into the room. "My aunt said you wanted me," she said, panting faintly.

Pippa patted her arm. "How many times do I have to tell you not to run up those stairs? I'm not going to scream if it takes you five minutes to get here, Nellie." She introduced the girl to Christiana, add-ing, "I'm going to take Christiana to the study for a while. I'll be up later to take over for you."

Nellie's eyes shone with admiration as she nodded. "I don't mind. I love taking care of the twins," she assured Pippa.

"And you're marvelous with them," Pippa replied warmly before gesturing Christiana out of the nursery.

Neither spoke as they went downstairs to the back of the house. Pippa led Christiana into a large room, paneled in light, pecky cypress with floor-to-ceiling windows.

"This is the only place in the house where I can

guarantee we won't be interrupted. Would you like coffee or something?''

Christiana shook her head as she took the chair across from Pippa.

''I told Marie to make certain you were aware of what you would be getting into if you decided to come to us. I won't mince words. That's not my way. Josh and I are very demanding. Josh is a busy man. As am I. When I'm writing I'm likely to forget that there is another person on the planet much less in the same house with me. We do a lot of entertaining, business as well as social. And a great deal of traveling.'' She smiled at Christiana's carefully attentive expression. ''So far I haven't said anything that makes us terribly impressive as parents, have I?''

Christiana had cut her adult teeth on diplomacy regardless of her personal feelings. ''You both are very established in your careers. That carries a lot of responsibility.''

''So does having children. The twins weren't accidents nor are they regretted for the demands they're making now. Josh and I love our children. This is where you come in and where all your predecessors have gone out. We want to be with our children every free minute. We want someone who will fit into the family, care for the twins as though they were theirs, and yet allow us the freedom to come and go as necessary, schedules and idiotic rules be damned. We need stability and flexibility. So far all we've had are marionettes or women hankering after Josh. My sister-in-law Lyla has friends to whom your agency has supplied nannies or au pairs, if you prefer. All of them are satisfied. I've met Marie and found her extremely professional and I haven't been at all pleased with the agency I've used in the past. I want someone special. Marie says you're the best.'' She paused, searching Christiana's face. ''Are you?'' she asked quietly.

Christiana recognized the challenge without any change of expression. ''*Best* is a hard description to live up to, and compared to whom? Am I better than Elsa or little Nellie. Yes. My training in England was extensive and I graduated at the top of my class. Am I the best nanny that ever lived? I have no idea, and for the most part I'm just too busy to care. I've never been fired from a job.'' She pulled a small list of references from her handbag and passed them to Pippa. ''You are at liberty to contact any one of those families. All have their bases in Europe, but I don't think you'll have any trouble reaching any of them.''

''You're very outspoken.''

Christiana smiled faintly. ''I don't think you're a person who would respect anything less.''

They studied each other for a moment, each probing for the strength of the other. Finally Pippa broke the silence.

''Why did you decide to come back to the States?''

''I was turning into a European. I didn't want that,'' Christiana returned simply.

Pippa opened the references and scanned the impressive list of names. The more she was exposed to this self-possessed woman, the more curious she felt. Yet none of her questions showed on her face as she lifted her eyes to Christiana. ''I think I'm going to like you very much," she decided, offering Christiana her hand. "And I know Josh is going to be delighted to have help at last."

Christiana cocked her head, liking the warmth of her new employer. "I have one question."

"Name it."

"When Marie called she mentioned some crisis had made finding a nanny today imperative. What was it?"

Pippa rose, her eyes sparkling with secrets and a desire to tease. "I think I'm going to pass on that one."

Christiana's lips twitched. Virgin she might be, but stupid she wasn't. There was something so blatantly sensual about Pippa's expression that she had no difficulty filling in the blanks. "That extra door in the nursery wouldn't be to your bedroom, would it?"

Pippa didn't even glance away. "It is."

Christiana wanted to swallow a laugh but couldn't. Pippa hadn't exaggerated. It was an unusual household indeed. She rose, her eyes alive with mischief. "Now that I'm here, maybe we can find a new place for the nursery. Children seldom pick appropriate moments to demand attention."

"Both Josh and I will second that opinion," Pippa agreed with feeling. "Tell me you can move in today and I'll be forever in your debt."

"I can," Christiana murmured, following her into the hall.

By the time the afternoon was over, Christiana had been given a guided tour, collected her belongings, and been installed in a large bedroom at the end of the hall which connected with another large bedroom that would soon have all of the twins' paraphernalia moved in. Her work in the Luck household had begun in flash of movement and laughter.

TWO

"Well, that's the lot. Thank you, Bridgette," Josh said, leaning back in his chair. "If you'll get those memos typed out this afternoon, you can take the rest of the day off. You worked hard last night. I really appreciate the overtime."

Bridgette smiled and collected her notepad. "I don't mind," she murmured before collecting the stack of mail they had just finished and leaving the room.

"I wish my secretary were as adept as Bridgette," Rich observed, getting to his feet to wander to the small bar in the far corner of the room. He opened the refrigerator and pulled out a vegetable juice. "Want something?"

"Seltzer and lime would be good." He watched while Rich fixed the drink. Had Josh been a woman he would have been impressed with the perfect symmetry of Rich's features. Tawny eyes in a face too handsome to be real glowed with intelligence and knowledge of mankind's faults and follies. Rich's six-foot-five-inch length was lean, muscular in the places a person could admire. His hair was a shade caught between gold and light brown, thick, with a wave that always found a way to fall over his brow. In short, Rich was impossibly attractive to the opposite sex and had a bank balance of inherited money and an old family name that made him a target for almost every eligible female within sight and hearing. When he was younger, Rich had indulged himself and enjoyed the women throwing themselves at him. Because the picking had been easy and the variety extensive, he had come away burned out from three marriages to partners more interested in what he had than what he was.

"I thought you liked Susan," Josh murmured mildly.

"I did until she decided to get amorous," he growled, turning to face Josh. "What is it with women? You'd think that the fact I've been married and divorced three times would put them off. It would me, if the positions were reversed." He stalked to Josh's desk and all but slammed his drink down.

Josh grinned. Having been friends with Rich for almost twelve years he knew how Rich's effect on the opposite sex rankled the younger man. "Most men would love to have your problem."

"Then they're fools. Having females drooling all over you just because of the way your body and face are put together is boring if not sickening. More than that it is a danger to what little peace I've managed to find in the last two years. This is the longest I've been single in my life and I don't ever intend to get tied up in the marriage knot again. Kay cured me of that fever forever."

Josh studied his friend's face, seeing the bitterness and pain that Rich felt safe enough to show him. "Not all women are like her."

Rich took a swallow of his drink and grimaced. "You couldn't prove it by me. Outside of Hollywood, I must have the world's worst record with women. The thing is, I like the idea of marriage. I just don't like the women I have to live with to enjoy it."

Josh chuckled appreciatively. "I could put Pippa on to finding you a mate. She has a damn good success rate."

Rich choked on his drink, his eyes molten gold in a face suddenly wiped clean of expression. "You let that wife of yours within a hundred miles of any woman that even looks like she might be interested in me and I'm leaving town and changing my name. I am not going to be on a list of candidates for that silver-haired witch. Just because you and Joe liked her matching doesn't mean I think much of it."

Josh sipped his drink, ignoring the bite of Rich's words. "It would almost be worth it just to see her in action again. Pippa has been too quiet of late. I think my life would be a lot easier if I gave her a diversion. Besides, you said yourself that you like the idea of marriage."

"Take her on a vacation to Antarctica," Rich returned promptly, avoiding addressing the last part of Josh's words.

Josh laughed. "No way. She doesn't have the wardrobe for it."

"You can afford a dozen wardrobes."

"Not the kind Pippa would buy." Visions of the abbreviated fashions that Pippa insisted were decent clothes danced in his head. His body, ever attuned to his thoughts, assisted the image with the proper response. He cursed silently and finished off his seltzer. Becoming aroused in his own office when Pippa wasn't even there was a bit over the top even for him. "Come to dinner tonight," he offered abruptly, needing a diversion.

"Why?" Rich demanded suspiciously. Josh looked as though he were up to something. Much as he liked and admired Pippa, the woman made him devoutly glad she was in love with Josh and not free to roam at will.

"To eat. What else?"

"How long have you been living with Pippa?" he asked, knowing exactly how long the unlikely pair had been married.

"Five years. Why?"

"Time enough to rub off," he muttered darkly, knowing he was going to accept. Pippa and Josh were the closest friends he had. Being around them was the next best thing to having a home and family of his own.

Josh shook his head, his eyes gleaming with amusement. "I leave that kind of thing strictly to Pippa. Just keeping up with her, the twins, and this business is more than enough for me."

Rich frowned, reminded of the information that had brought him barging into Josh's afternoon dictation. "I need to talk to you about the fuel project."

Josh was quick to note the change of tone. He sobered. "Trouble?"

"It looks that way." Damn, he hated unsubstantiated rumors, especially of this magnitude. "Our new synthetic fuel formula and the prototype burner are being talked about in certain quarters, the wrong quarters. Where it's being developed and how far along the project is, is being reported with entirely too much accuracy for it to be coincidental. With the final tests and analysis still pending for a patent, we can't afford these kinds of leaks."

"How's the word getting out? Gossip or something closer to home?"

"I think closer to home. Inside even." Rich watched the words sink in, felt the same kind of controlled anger he could see on Josh's face. The company had worked long and hard to put the new idea into practical form. Years of frustration and disappointment had brought them to the edge of an earth-changing development. Now that they were so close, their security, something that they had been able to count on without fail, seemed to be compromised.

"It could be a plant to make us change things, to create a crack in the wall that doesn't exist now. But I don't think so. My source is too good to be that far off. I think the word really is on the streets that we're on to something of major importance. There are also whispers of a foreign buyer and an unlimited purse. Where there is big money there will be people around to risk anything."

Josh's features tightened, endless possibilities of industrial espionage, sabotage, and various other delaying tactics without the probability of theft tearing through his thoughts. "*Foreign* could be anyone born in Canada to the Middle East. Can't you be more specific?"

"I wish I could. The information just came my way this morning. I haven't had time to do more than make a few phone calls to confirm the existence of the talk. Right now most of it is underground. But we can't hope to keep it that way. We've been lucky to keep everything under wraps this long."

"Hell!"

"My sentiments and then some. How do you want to proceed?"

Josh stared through Rich as he considered his options and his assets, of which Rich was at the top of the list. Officially, Rich bore the title of vice president of Luck Enterprises. The truth was far more complex. Josh knew himself to be the brains behind the development of his company, but Rich filled a multifaceted role of troubleshooter, able to turn his hand at anything from assisting in the settlement of a labor dispute to investigation of industrial espionage. Right now it was the latter talent on which Josh depended. "Start with the usual stuff. Background checks on everyone in the company, concentrating on those employed by the two developmental plants. I don't want anyone left out, including you and me. I trust both of us, but it could be someone close to us that we would miss otherwise. Set up a secondary security team to oversee the first."

Rich nodded, having already done some thinking of his own and come to the same conclusions. "Anything else?"

"I want you to see to it personally. Until this mess is cleared up, delegate anything you're working on to someone else."

"I was hoping you would say that." He smiled in a way that would have terrified the culprit had he or she been present. "I definitely like the way you think."

Josh echoed his smile, his eyes deadly serious. "I trust you to protect our investment, the formula, and the prototype. Use whatever means you deem appropriate."

"I can't believe how quiet it has been today. I can't wait to see Josh's face when he finds out you're here already," Pippa said, sinking onto the lounge chair beside the pool. "I actually managed to get some work done. How did you convince the twins it was time for their nap? The minute they turned three they assured me they were too old for the practice."

Christiana lay on the lounge next to Pippa. Lazily opening one eye, she smiled faintly. "Magic and bribery."

Pippa chuckled, enjoying the unexpected plus of Christiana's sense of humor. She studied the taller woman without seeming to. Once unwrapped from its concealing shroud of clothing, the body stretched its length at her side was definitely riveting. *Wrap* being the operative word. So far Pippa had seen her in two different outfits, not counting the swimsuit. Both had been cut fully, allowing nothing of the wearer's figure to show to advantage.

"Now why didn't I think of that?" She eyed Christiana, this time with open appreciation. Never one to leave her curiosity unsatisfied, Pippa risked a question. "Why on earth do you wear those bulky clothes? You've got a gorgeous figure."

Christiana looked at her, searching her expression, debating the merits of the truth versus her usual response. The sincerity in Pippa's gaze, the understanding, decided her. "Camouflage," Christiana replied simply, then waited.

Pippa looked her over once more, then nodded. "Groping men who think with their hormones instead of their minds are a pain. Being in a live-in situation can't be much help, either."

"It isn't," Christiana agreed, relaxing when she hadn't realized she was tense. "I was very young when I started in this business. I'd heard stories, of course, but youth has an ability to shut its ears to anything. I quickly learned the dangers of being built like this. Knocking some fool down the back stairs has quite a number of drawbacks. So I reinstated the disguise philosophy that had seen me through school. I figured if it worked with a bunch of overactive adolescents, then it would do the trick in the present and the future. It did. I breathe easier these days. Of course, not being beautiful helps." The last was added without a trace of bitterness. "Plus being able to look down on male heads adds to the camouflage. Six-foot-tall women are still in the minority."

"And three-quarters of that are legs I would die for."

Christiana stared. Having expected the word big, the usual description applied to women of her proportions, to pop out in the conversation somewhere, she had difficulty believing that nothing but admiration glowed in Pippa's extraordinary eyes.

"How have you managed to stay single all this time? Or is there a divorce in your past?"

"No divorce and no one I was interested in asked," Christiana responded honestly.

"You must know an awful lot of blind and dumb

men. Of course, not every man is strong like my Josh . . or Alex . . . or Jason.''

Christiana chuckled, turning on her back to lie face up. "The first one I recognize, but who are the second and third?"

Pippa rolled on her side. "Most people would have thought they were my lovers. Why didn't you?"

"Wrong tone in your voice. There's affection but no desire."

Pippa thought that over, startled at the quick ear and the intuitive mind she had discovered. "What other talents are you hiding under that calm exterior?"

Christiana nodded toward the board casting a long shadow over them from across the pool. "That."

Pippa glanced over her shoulder. "But you haven't used it yet. You're not even wet."

Christiana shifted restlessly. "I rarely dive for an audience." She sat up, turning to Pippa, her gaze unknowingly defensive.

"How early did you bloom?" Pippa asked gently.

"Too damn early for the emotions I needed," Christiana answered frankly.

"Kids can be cruel."

"The Marquis de Sade was a gentleman compared to the group I knew." Christiana shrugged, not wanting to remember those years of cruel remarks to a girl too soon in a woman's body. "It's gotten better but never really gone away."

Pippa rose gracefully and collected her hat and sunglasses.

Startled, Christiana looked up.

"What time do you usually dive and for how long?"

"Six A.M. An hour."

"Then keep that time. It works perfectly for us. I hate mornings anyway. And if the twins get up, Josh or I will get them."

Touched, especially knowing about the crisis that precipitated her hiring, Christiana started to protest. "I can't let you do that . . ."

"You can't stop me from deciding your time off. I also employ you." Her smile softened the firm words. "The only other one who might see you is Elsa, and she doesn't even speak to Josh at that time of the morning." She turned, heading for the French doors leading to the lanai. "As for today, I'm going in. My new story is beating on my brain to be let out. Have to answer the call of the muse or the contrary flirt will leave me in the lurch. If you want to practice, the pool is yours." Without another word, Pippa left her alone.

Christiana gazed after her, torn between laughter at the rather gentle ruthlessness of her employer and tears for the soft heart and kindness that had given her the gift of solitude. She hadn't expected such simple and easy acceptance. Her eyes thoughtful, Christiana slipped off the lounger, out of her coverup, and walked around the pool to the board. As she mounted the ladder, she considered the home which was easier by the moment to think of as her own. Even the dour Elsa had a kind of hypnotic effect. Now if the absent Josh would live up to his advance notices, she would be able to settle for a while. After the ambassador's family, she had expected to work through a number of situations before she found a place she really liked. This stint with the Lucks didn't have the travel and diplomatic challenge of the last post, but it certainly couldn't be termed ordinary or dull. Smiling, she poised on the edge of the platform, her body flexed for the first dive, her swan.

Pippa glanced out the window of her writing room, watching as Christiana stroked to the side of the pool. Her silvery brows drew together in a frown of concentration as she watched Christiana rise out of the water, the yellow suit molded to her body so faithfully that no one could have mistaken her splendid proportions. "Josh will kill me," she muttered to herself. "But there is no way I can let that creature spend the rest of her life alone. There must be a man around with a mind to appreciate what she is and enough control over his hormones not to make a grab for her in a dark corner." As Christiana remounted the ladder, Pippa mentally reviewed her list of candidates. One of her favorites was Martin Richland, but his experience with his looks was almost as traumatic as Christiana's had been. "That could be a blessing," she mumbled, her lips curving into a smile Josh would have recognized and for which he would have threatened to lock her up and throw away the key. "I have been good. I haven't touched matchmaking in almost five years. I might get rusty. Of course, if I get Christiana a mate, we'll have to look for a new nanny." That prospect brought a frown which cleared a moment later. "This time I'll send to England."

The phone rang, startling her. She answered, smiling when she heard Josh's voice. "I do so love it when you call me during the day," she whispered in her best bedroom drawl. His groan made her laugh huskily.

"Woman, behave. Rich is in the office and I'll be damned if I'm going to explain the effect you have on my anatomy to him. I called to ask you if dinner can go to three. I thought I would bring him home with me."

Pippa glanced to the ceiling, knowing that Fate had just given its seal of approval to her half-formed plans. "It will stretch perfectly. Besides, we have something to celebrate. I found a nanny. And we are moving the twins down the hall."

"I think I like this nanny already." Talking with Pippa always made the day better. "Now tell me I won't find her staring at me and I may even give her a raise."

Pippa glanced out the window. "Oh, I can definitely guarantee you'll be safe in that department," she agreed, keeping the laughter from her voice. Giving Josh a hint of what she was up to wasn't in the cards right yet. "Go back to work, darling, so I can. Tell Rich I said hi."

Josh hung up, still smiling. Rich watched, conscious of the unrelenting loneliness of his life and an envy for the love and the special relationship Pippa and Josh shared. Josh was lucky in finding what he himself had sought futilely all his life.

"It seems Pip has done the impossible again. She has found us a new nanny."

"Starched up matron with Marine drill-sergeant tendencies or nubile female looking for a husband?"

"I don't think either from the way Pippa sounds. We'll find out tonight."

Rich grimaced. "I think I would rather skip it until you know for sure."

Josh tipped back his head, laughing. "I'd forgotten about Beth," he said, eyeing Rich's irritated expression. "I wonder if women have any idea how difficult it is for a man to escape a determined female's advances?"

"That crazy girl had more hands than a damn octopus and she was hardly big enough to breathe deeply. If Pippa hadn't walked in on us that night, I would have had to hurt her to escape with what little virtue I had intact."

"Instead you had to suffer through bedroom looks and sighs for the rest of the evening."

"I thought I was past the age of being embarrassed, but Beth made me rethink my belief. I was sure glad when you and Pippa let her go."

"We figured it was the only way we would ever get you back in the house again."

"I don't know how you stood it."

"She didn't bother me once she got a look at that pretty-boy face of yours."

Rich scowled. Josh grinned. Rich shook his head, his lips twitching with suppressed amusement. "You know I hate that description."

"Then you should have plastic surgery to take care of the problem."

"Or wear a paper bag." Rich got to his feet. "This is an inane conversation that is wasting time better spent getting on that security problem."

Josh inclined his head, his expression somber. "I don't need to tell you to keep me informed."

Rich nodded before leaving as silently as he had come.

* * *

"You want me to do what?" Christiana turned, J. Jr.'s shirt dangling from her hands. Pippa's innocent expression couldn't be faulted. Christiana couldn't think why she didn't trust it one inch.

"Come down to dinner with Josh and a friend of his from work. I hate uneven numbers and I think you'll like Rich." Pippa lifted her daughter in her arms, smiling as the little girl tucked her face against her neck.

"I'd rather not. I don't really have anything with me for a dinner with your husband's friends." Her excuse was a small exaggeration, but Pippa couldn't know that she always kept at least one reasonably dressy garment with her—just in case.

"How do you know? You haven't even met Rich. He's one of the easiest-going men I've ever met, and clothes don't impress him at all. In fact, if you went to a lot of trouble you'd probably break him out in a terminal case of hives."

Startled, Christiana studied Pippa carefully. "Why?" she asked baldly.

Pippa kissed Lori's cheek, loving the closeness of her child but using it, too. Christiana was probably the most wary woman she had ever met. Getting her into a receptive mood for a man like Rich would take delicate handling. "Rich, or Martin Richland III, has a rather blatant problem."

Curious at Pippa's wording, Christiana forgot her own caution long enough to take the first nibble on the bait. "What kind of problem?"

"He's beautiful. Sexy as sin, actually. Wealthy— old money—and he's got the kind of personality that makes a woman feel like she's the only one in the room."

"That's a problem?" Christiana's brows rose higher with every compliment to the unknown Rich.

"It is if you're a romantic and an idealist. He's both. I think the phrase 'poor little rich girl' could be paraphrased to include him. From what Josh tells me, the man had a family that could have given ice cubes heat. He's been married three times, and every one was a disaster. He's been burned so many times he doesn't want to play with fire ever again." Pippa put Lori down onto the rug. Without being obvious she scanned Christiana's face. The curiosity reflected there was tempered by wariness. Satisfied with the seeds she had planted, she ruffled her son's hair, laughing at the groan of a young male's disdain. "So take pity on me with two men to entertain and join us. I promise you Rich won't chase you around the table, and I know he'll be safe with you."

THREE

Christiana surveyed herself in the mirror, frowning at the soft folds of delicate cotton flowing from her shoulders in a concealing web of pink, lavender, and cream. The dress had been designed by a friend in England as a kind of at-home lounge outfit. Christiana had fallen in love with the colors as much as with the figure-hiding lines. Tonight she wasn't sure she liked either. She had just come from putting the children down for the evening and had passed Pippa on the way downstairs on Josh's arm. Admittedly she had noticed her employer's briefly cut clothes during the day. She had assumed that Pippa's attire was dictated by comfort not intent, but after seeing what Pippa was wearing tonight, she wasn't certain her assessment had been accurate. The tissue-gauze outfit had been a designer's dream in construction, seeming to defy the laws of nature to stay in place. It would take something extraordinary for an ordinary woman to even begin to make her presence felt in

Pippa's company. She frowned as the unusual thought intruded. She didn't compete, never had. Yet . . .

The lines on her brow deepened as she stared at her image. Just once she would like to be as at home with her physical attributes as Pippa was. Just once she would like to wear something not intended to hide her figure but rather to embrace and cling to its lines. Startled at the need she had thought dead if not buried, she turned from her reflection. She knew she wasn't the kind of woman to take the comments her body always provoked. She knew she didn't want to go back to fighting for her virtue, and she knew life was much simpler, less painful if she stayed within the boundaries she had set for herself. Smoothing her expression, she left the room and the mirror behind. She was who and what she was. Wishing for different wouldn't make her life any more fulfilling than it was. She had chosen her course. It wasn't perfect, but it was a lot better than some. For a moment, she remembered the story Pippa had told her about Martin Richland. If she hadn't decided to play it safe, his history might have been hers. She shuddered delicately, finding her sympathy caught by the man she had yet to meet. At least this time she wouldn't have to run for cover. He was probably no more eager to put his head on the emotional chopping block than she. Feeling a little better about the dress and her fade-into-the-woodwork image, she descended the stairs.

"You look fabulous as usual, Pippa," Rich said, smiling into his hostess's pale eyes as he took her hand and lifted it to his lips. The gesture had become a ritual between them.

Pippa patted his cheek, playing the game. "You don't think it's too daring." She flicked him a wicked glance out of eyes created to tease.

He laughed, shaking his head as he released her hand. "It's a good thing Josh knows I'm scared to death of you or he'd have my head."

Josh handed him a drink as he slipped an arm around his misbehaving wife. "Woman, just this once, pretend you're a lady."

She laughed, molding her side to his. "Why? Rich would be certain I had something up my sleeve—"

"You never wear them, at least not in the evening," Josh interrupted with a grin that admired the satin skin showing above the deep cut of the bodice of her white gown.

Pippa ignored the comment. "And you would be sending for the doctor to find out if I was sick."

Rich lifted his glass to her. Pippa was an intriguing woman who seemed created to spin webs of humor, mischief, and chaos. While he enjoyed watching her lead Josh a merry life, he had no desire for such a mate for himself. "She's got you there, my friend."

"I never should have gone on that cruise."

Tipping his head, Rich laughed. "I'm glad I didn't. Having you and Joe come back married sent every bachelor around here into a spin. No one thought either of you would ever do it."

Christiana entered the room on the last words. She paused in the doorway, watching the occupants who, as yet, hadn't seen her. Without realizing it, she inhaled sharply as Martin Richland angled his head so that the light fell over his profile. Pippa hadn't exaggerated. He was beautiful and his voice had the smoothness of aged brandy and the kick of white lightning. His laugh was the kind that invited others to share his enjoyment, and for the second time in as many hours here was a man who didn't make her feel as though she had stumbled into a land of midgets.

"Oh, there you are, Christiana," Pippa said, sliding out of Josh's reach to move toward her. "Come and meet Rich and let Josh get you a drink. I'm having white wine. I can't stand sherry."

Rich studied the new arrival, expecting to be able to dismiss her after the first cursory inspection. At first glance she seemed to possess little physical beauty. Her face was mildly pleasant, but her body, what he could see of it, was built along splendidly lush lines. She wasn't young, yet if he had been asked, he wouldn't have been able to place her age. There was something about her that defied description. For a fleeting second as he looked into Christiana's eyes, he remembered the woman he had watched dive that morning. His swan had had that same poise, that sense of awareness that he saw in Christiana's expression. Startled, he looked closer. His swan, too, had been tall. There the similarity ended. His diver had been at home with her body, clearly knowing its perfection to the last ounce. This woman seemed uneasy with hers, given more to hiding than striding through the world with grace and delicacy.

Without realizing it, he breathed a sigh of relief. At least this nanny had no interest in husband-hunting. The evening could be enjoyed after all, he decided.

"White wine will be fine," Christiana said, turning her head so that she wasn't looking into Rich's eyes as he took her measure. She had always been sensitive to undercurrents, and the room was filled with them. Pippa was watching her expectantly, Martin was still gazing at her as though he wasn't certain what to make of her; and Josh looked resigned, even faintly amused.

"This is Martin Richland the Third," Pippa announced as one pulling a purebred rabbit from a hat. "Rich, this is Christiana Drake, the wonder woman brave enough to take on me, this house, Elsa, and the twins."

Christiana took the glass Josh passed her, smiling at Pippa. "Someone had to rescue you," she murmured. "That frog looked interested in attack."

Pippa laughed, tucking her arm into the crook of Josh's. "I definitely was off balance today." She ignored her husband's snort of laughter. "It's a good thing Christiana has nerves of steel or we would never have gotten to the interview stage at all."

Rich looked from one woman to the other, finding their shared amusement contagious. The flash of gentle humor in Christiana's eyes surprised him with the way it lit her face, adding a glow to her pale skin. "I'm intrigued. What about the frog," he said, watching Christiana, feeling as though he were seeing a flower opening to the first touch of the morning sun. As she moved nearer, her scent wrapped around him, a delicate mesh of fragrance that teased his senses and urged him closer. When her eyes flickered briefly in his direction he caught a fleeting glimpse of the same awareness that he was feeling. Stunned, Rich took a sip of his drink. After all the beautiful women of his past, how could this one, especially now, slip past his guard. She wasn't pretty. She definitely wasn't created along the more slender lines he favored and she was in the upper levels of the age he usually dated. Lost in his thoughts, he hardly noticed Pippa urging them through the open French doors to the garden before taking up her tale. He moved closer, looking for something special about her to explain his surprising reaction. Using Pippa's outrageously embellished story as a connection, he murmured, "I don't think she knows what the truth is." Her eyes were wonderful, clear, bright, and yet strangely shy. But the more he studied her the more convinced he became that he knew her. And yet with his memory for faces, he couldn't think how. His curiosity touched on two counts, he ignored all the reasons he had learned for steering clear of the opposite sex.

"If I hadn't been there, I wouldn't have recognized the story," Christiana admitted, looking at him fully for the first time. His gaze was like liquid gold pouring warmth over her. Without either one of them realizing it, their steps slowed, allowing the older couple to pull ahead.

Rich stopped, angling his body on the brick walk so that Christiana had to stop as well. "I swear I've seen you somewhere before," he said, searching her face, fighting the sense of familiarity that was growing by the second.

"I would have remembered. Your coloring is very distinctive. Besides, unless you have been wandering around Europe for the last few years there is no way we could have met."

Rich frowned. "Have you family in the area?"

She smiled, wondering at his persistence. "No," she replied calmly, sipping her wine.

"Do you dive?" he asked abruptly, a farfetched notion taking root in his mind.

Christiana hid her surprise with only the smallest of hesitation. Instinct warned her to tread carefully. Her expression smoothed, no hint of her sudden disquiet marred the ivory perfection of her skin. "Skindive? No."

His hand sliced the air in a gesture of frustration that he rarely permitted himself to show. There was no way Christiana and his diver could be the same woman and yet he wanted to make the connection. "Not skin-dive. High dive."

"Why do you ask?" she parried.

"You remind me of someone I know who dives, and beautifully as a matter of fact." He waited, not certain even now which answer he hoped she returned.

"And you don't know what she looks like?" Her brows rose considering the odds of him knowing about her diving. "Odd." As unlikely as it appeared, Rich had to have been her audience at the school pool. There was no other way he could have known.

Rich shrugged, wishing he had never started the conversation. There was no way Christiana and his diver could be the same woman. The mess with the formula had him close to distraction. That was all. "Forget it. Obviously I mistook you for someone else." He nodded toward Pippa and Josh, who had stopped a few yards ahead. "Shall we join the others?"

Josh leaned next to Pippa's ear. "Wife of mine, I ought to wring your gorgeous neck. Rich isn't a man who is going to take it nicely that you're trying to arrange his life. Especially about this. Kay did a number on him that he'll never forget. And your candidate doesn't look the type to handle the kind of hurt Rich can dish out when he's cornered.''

Pippa leaned into his side, laying her head on his shoulder. "Only someone as damaged as Rich will understand him. My instincts tell me that Christiana could be that woman.''

Josh looked at her sternly. "I have great respect for those instincts of yours, but if you're wrong, they'll both be hurt. And so will you. Your heart is too tender for this kind of meddling.'' He hugged her to him.

Pippa touched his cheek. "I'm not meddling. You know me better than that. This is as far as. I go. From here it's up to them unless one or both ask for help.'' She smiled into his troubled eyes. "Trust me.''

"You know I do.'' Josh glanced at Rich and Christiana as he and Pippa walked toward them. "They do look good together. Her height and his match well. She's not beautiful, but that has never mattered to Rich. And she likes children, which definitely does make a difference.''

Pippa smiled softly. "See. I'm not so crazy. Want to bet on the outcome?'' Her silver brows arched in a feminine challenge.

Josh looked down at his wife, reading the dare in her eyes. "Woman, I should have run a mile the first time I saw you on that plane.''

"Think of all the fun you would have missed.''

He groaned, thinking of all the peace he didn't miss. Pippa was a delightful handful, who, he was convinced, lay awake nights thinking of ways to drive him to distraction. "All right. I'll bite. What are the stakes to this little wager?"

"A Maserati."

Josh studied his wife. "Over my dead body. You drive nearly as badly as you cook. You'd kill yourself."

She laughed huskily, patting his cheek. "Scared I'm right?"

Josh recognized the trap and walked in anyway. Male honor had to be upheld, after all. "All right, you're on. But what do I get?"

"Anything you want," she offered magnanimously.

Surprised, he turned back to Rich and Christiana. When Pippa was that certain, Josh knew he had a damn good shot at having his crazy wife running around Jacksonville in a racy, four-wheeled bomb.

"And no fair warning Rich. Not that it will do much good."

Josh's head jerked back to his wife's laughing face. "You told him?"

"No. How could I? You've been with us every moment since you came home. Instincts, my love. You remember. You used to have them before I showed you you didn't need them around me. I would protect you from all those little girls who aspired to your bed."

Josh kissed her hard, a punishment or an agreement. Even he wasn't sure which. "Damn you, woman. I know I should have stayed home that day. You don't get better with age; you get worse."

"If you live around those two for long, you had better get used to their affection for each other,"

Rich said dryly, slanting a glance at Christiana's face.

"It's refreshing."

"It also has a way of making a man like me envious," he said without thinking.

Christiana looked at him, stunned at the sudden depth of emotion in his voice.

Rich met her eyes, shrugging. "Forget I said that." The compassion in her eyes was mesmerizing. His hand lifted, his fingers almost reaching the softness of her cheek. Then he remembered who he was and all the reasons why he couldn't let his emotions run free. His hand dropped as his expression smoothed. Tonight was proving to be a very unsettling evening. "Why don't we go in? They'll follow in a while."

Christiana had seen the vulnerability in his expression before he had wiped it clean. With the information that Pippa had given her, she had no difficulty in understanding the pain of his past. His gesture had surprised her, but oddly, she had almost welcomed his touch. She certainly hadn't thought about drawing away. Her response bothered her. Being drawn to a man with his reputation was a shock. "All right," she murmured, no more eager to share any more of the moonlight with Rich than he was with her.

Christiana woke up the next morning at the usual five A.M. but minus the feeling of having slept well and deeply. Rich's image would not leave her alone. Throughout dinner the night before she had caught fleeting glimpses of a gentler more approachable man. His sense of humor and intelligence had shown in the table conversation, his caring for Pippa and Josh restrained but clear. Yet with her, there had been an aloofness, a distance all the more telling for its simple neutrality. The moments in the garden might have been a dream. More than indifference, his attitude had stoked the fire of her own curiosity about the man, challenging her as no male had ever done. She smiled grimly as she pulled on a green one-piece.

"I've got rocks for brains," she muttered. "I ought to be glad he's ignoring me so carefully instead of acting like a child deprived of a promised toy."

She grabbed her towel and robe, shrugging into the latter as she stepped into the hall. She took a moment to check on the twins, who were sleeping like the angels they weren't before going downstairs. For the second day in a row she needed the mind-taming concentration of her diving. Only this time the image of a man, not her own need for a physical renewal, drove her. As she slipped into the pool, she glanced over her shoulder, half expecting to find Rich watching from the windows of the salon.

"Damn," she swore uncharacteristically when she realized what she was doing. Striking out for the far side of the coping, she slammed the lid on her wandering thoughts. She would not allow Rich to disturb her again. He had made the rules and they suited her very well. She wanted no man in any capacity in her future.

Rich pulled on his jogging shorts, knowing he really needed a good run this morning. The evening before should have been relaxing, but he felt tense and restless instead, as though something important had shifted in his world. Irritated with himself and the woman who had sat so calmly across from him at the table, he was in no mood to be thwarted by anyone or anything. To arrive at the school and discover the pool that had held such eye-riveting grace and beauty the day before was as calm as that woman's eyes spurred his already uncertain temper.

"Damn," he swore irritably. He hadn't even realized how much he had wanted to see the unknown diver again. Her perfection had been a joy to behold, and the freedom of her flight from sky to water made dreams seem possible. He stood staring at the emptiness, making no attempt to begin his run. He was waiting for her. He knew it, didn't understand it, but accepted it. When a half hour passed without any other sign of life, he knew she would not come. Sighing, he turned away, disappointed, curious and knowing that he would return tomorrow to find her. Odd, he thought as he warmed up. He couldn't have described her face if asked, but he would have been able to pick out her body in a host of others if he had to. He grinned at the thought as he began his run. Even as he pictured the regal grace of her flight, hope drowned out his disappointment. He refused to believe his swan wouldn't return tomorrow. And when she did, he would be waiting. This time he would talk to her, see her face, know the sound of her voice.

Josh scanned the preliminary security checks that Rich had just laid on his desk. "I don't see anything here to indicate any kind of security breach."

"Neither do I," Rich said abruptly, his eyes narrowed on the papers he had almost committed to memory. "Of course, that is just the top layer, information we've been over at the point of employment.

I'm still working on the in-depth financial searches on the employees and their families. We'll have a lot more by the end of the week."

"I didn't expect us to turn up the culprit right away. He or she has to be good or they wouldn't have gotten this far without detection. But I had hoped for some leads. Even little ones."

Rich got up, his movements tense, frustrated. "I had thought so, too. It seems incredible that anyone could have gotten to us after all the precautions we've taken."

Josh watched Rich pace. "What else is bothering you?"

"I can't shake the feeling that we're looking in the wrong place."

Josh's brows rose, but he said nothing, letting Rich think aloud.

"With very few exceptions everyone connected with both projects has been with the company since its beginning. That's why you handpicked the locations. Even the security people involved are old-timers."

"Money can buy a lot."

"I don't need the reminder. But usually there is a need somewhere to be met."

"Maybe there will be something in the financial checks that our prelims missed."

Rich shrugged, his muscles clenching in sympathy with his temper. "Maybe we ought to lock down the sites."

Josh's expression smoothed as he considered the idea. "Put the projects on hold? That will throw our completion schedule right down the toilet. I'm not sure that definite a move is called for at this point."

"True, but locking up the material, the formulas, and the prototype will be a strategy that won't be expected because they'll be as aware of the delay factor as we are. We've made no bones about our eagerness to get the fuel into production. And the timing, as we all know, couldn't be better. Our villain won't like the plan and that may make him careless. Plus his greed is an added spur. We would have a better chance of nailing him in a controlled, closed environment."

"All good points, but I still don't like the lost time." Josh leaned back in his chair, thinking. "Someone else could beat us to the market. We can't even be sure that they are actually after the formula. It could be a trick to get us to try just what you're suggesting. Someone out there could be as close to a solution as we are. None of us needs reminding that the first one in with the patent is the holder of potential millions of dollars in revenue."

"Agreed." Rich flung himself into a chair, moving his hand in a sharp arc. "It's your company and your decision—potentially your loss or gain. I'll implement whichever course you choose."

"I don't like being scared into a choice."

"Neither do I."

"We'll wait, long enough for your security checks to come through, then reassess."

Rich nodded as he rose to leave. "I'll keep you posted."

FOUR

Christiana cast a look over the twins as they settled down for their midday nap. She smiled a little as she considered the newest of her homes. Josh and Pippa were truly caring parents and their children's natures reflected the stability the unusual household provided. Pippa and Josh had shared an hour after breakfast with Lori and J. Jr. before each had begun the day. Josh had left for the office and Pippa had retreated to the room at the back of the house that overlooked the river. Elsa had provided breakfast for the twins to the tune of infrequent grunts that passed as conversation. Other than those short moments, Christiana arranged her own time. And now, for the next hour or so, she could please herself. Lori gave her a sleepy smile before plopping her thumb between her pink lips. Christiana smoothed her pale curls against the round head, her lips unknowingly echoing Lori's innocent expression. When she was sure the twins were safely asleep, Christiana tidied

the nursery and left the room. Needing a little adult
activity, she put on her swimsuit and made her way
down to the pool. Pippa still hadn't emerged from
her writing retreat, so she was alone. Christina
slipped out of her short robe and dove into the pool
from the edge of the coping. The water was deli-
ciously cool and invigorating a she stroked the length
in a lazy crawl. She was on her third trip when she
suddenly felt as though someone was watching. She
halted midway, treading water as she scanned the
area. At first she didn't see Rich as he stood in the
shadow of the lanai.

Rich stared at the woman sliding through the
water. For the first few seconds he didn't recognize
Christiana. Her wet hair was darker, richer in color.
Her skin was pale and her long length definitely was
anything but overweight. Her movements were grace
personified. Had her feet been a long silvery tail he
could not have thought her environment more perfectly suited to her. A frown marred his brow. Once
again he thought of his diver. He moved in the sunlight, his eyes tracing her body as she moved gently
in front of him. The water rippled about her making
it impossible to define her figure.

"You're very good," he murmured quietly, searching her eyes, looking for some sign of the same kind
of confusion that clouded his thinking whenever he
was near her. All he saw was his own reflection.

"I like to swim," Christiana replied, staying as
low as possible. Her behavior of the day before
seemed like a dream. How she could have performed
for those all-seeing golden eyes defied her imagina-

tion. Even now, she felt as though she wore nothing between her skin and his gaze but water.

Rich sat down on the lounger over which Christiana had thrown her wrap. "Swim team?"

Christiana wanted to curl her arms about her breasts, protecting the fullness from the tracing of his look. But more than that, she wanted him gone. "No."

Her negative response startled him, but not nearly as much as the finality with which she spoke. His curiosity aroused, he remarked, "You look like you were good enough. Why not?"

"Not interested. And why are you?" Staying neutral when one was treading water was nearly impossible, Christiana found. She eyed her robe, wishing she dared leave the security of the concealing water. A breeze had come up from the river, sliding over the surface of the pool in a way that was like standing straight from a warm shower in front of an air-conditioner vent. Christiana shivered.

Rich frowned. He picked up the towel that lay beside him and got to his feet. "You're cold. Why don't you come out?"

Another gust of wind darted across Christiana's bare shoulders. "I will when you leave," she said, cold enough not to bother with a polite evasion. At that moment the sun decided to hide behind a cloud. What heat had been available left with the light.

Rich stared at her, unable to believe her reply. "I beg your pardon," he murmured blankly.

Christiana gritted her teeth against their need to chatter. "I said when you leave, I'll get out," she muttered, feeling more vulnerable and more foolish by the moment.

"Good Lord, woman. What century did you say you were born in? I thought that tent you were wearing last night was a bit odd, but this is ridiculous. Believe me, the sight of your body isn't likely to drive me to ravage you. For one thing I've learned discrimination in my maturity."

Christiana's temper did a slow burn. It didn't help that he was right about her behavior. "Discrimination." The word carried the sizzle of a hot poker plunged into a cold bath. "I couldn't care less about your discrimination. I just want my privacy, and if you were any kind of a gentleman, you would go away."

Rich might have done just that, but curiosity was one of his failings and this woman had managed to bother him more in his short acquaintance than any female had in a long time. "I know you're in the wrong century for sure. Being a gentlemen these days only lays a man open for a lot of smart remarks." He spread the towel between his hands, flaring it as a bullfighter would when facing a charge. Challenge was a fire in his eyes. "I'm not going. I wonder which is worse, me seeing you or a good cold?"

Christiana eyed him and her towel. Paybacks were hell, she reminded herself. He would have his. Her eyes fixed on his, she stroked to him. She stopped a few inches from the edge and raised her hands. Her dare was no less potent than his.

Rich studied her. "If you pull me in, so help me, I'll tan your backside."

Christiana smiled, her intent losing none of its strength.

Rich tossed the towel over the chair, just in case.

Bracing himself, he reached down. Their hands locked. He hesitated, expecting her weight against his. When she only hung there, his brows lifted in surprise. Flexing his muscles, he lifted up. As the water released Christiana from its gentle embrace, Rich got a view of the woman that no picture could have done justice.

"My God!" he breathed reverently. The water line lapped at Christiana's hips as he paused, holding her suspended between sky and pool. Forgetting everything he had ever learned about leverage, he shifted his weight. The next few seconds were a slow-motion reel of a man's unscheduled nosedive. Christiana slid under the surface, the image of Rich's stunned face etched forever in her mind. She had almost pulled him in, but at the last she had known she couldn't have her revenge that way. As she popped to the top, she looked around for her nemesis. A second later, his face appeared inches from her own.

"You aren't fat," he announced, seemingly oblivious to the water pouring off his hair.

It was impossible not to smile at his unconcealed shock. "No."

"Why in the devil do you hide that kind of body under that damn tent? It's a crime against nature."

Christiana's smile slid into oblivion as she subtly drew away from him. "My profession has a few drawbacks. Add my dimensions to the pot and you have a brew created for trouble. I don't like trouble. So I avoid the situation to the best of my ability."

Rich frowned, unable to believe the calm with which she spoke. It didn't take much of a stretch of his imagination to read between the lines. She was sensitive. He had known it last night. There was something fragile about her as well, something easily damaged under too much pressure. He didn't want to think about the kind of problems with which she had had to cope just because of the gene mix that had produced a body so beautiful. Without realizing it, he reached out a hand to her.

Christiana looked at it, then raised her eyes to his. "Pity?"

"Compassion. I have my own cross to bear." With the hand he would have given her, he touched his face. "Between this and my money, I've lived through my own share of misconceptions. They have a way of toughening some of us. Others go into hiding."

Christiana searched his expression, finding no lies, only truth. The breeze quickened again. She shivered. "Like me."

He tread water closer to her. "Yes. You shouldn't let the world cram you into a corner. You lose part of yourself to a bunch of fools who won't even appreciate the gift."

His words sank gently into her soul, sliding past barriers she had spent most of her life erecting. This time it was her hand that reached out, her eyes that spoke silently of compassion. "You do understand," she murmured.

Rich shifted restlessly, having no more liking for her sight than she had for his. He had his own shields and they were shaking. He turned his head, looking away from her hand and her gentleness. "Let's get out of here. I don't know about you, but I'm turning into an ice cube." Without touching her, he struck out for the side of the pool.

Understanding the abrupt switch of mood, Christiana hesitated. She had gotten too close. Had he shouted it, she couldn't have felt the effect of his rejection more profoundly. Stroking slowly to the side, she mentally pulled away from the tie they had begun to forge. She looked up at him, standing straight and tall above her. His face could have been carved by a master sculptor, its beauty so complete. But his heart and soul, like her own, were riddled with damage and pain. Suddenly she knew she wouldn't be able to bear his touch. Before he could help her, she levered herself up and out. It was then that Rich realized who she was. He had seen his swan slide out of her pool with just that move. It was too distinctive to belong to two different women.

"I do know you," he said the moment she stood beside him.

Christiana paused in the act of drying her hair. She neither looked away from the accusation in his eyes nor did she react to the verbal challenge. She simply waited.

Rich shook his head, sending droplets of water flashing in the hide-and-seek sunlight. "I was at the school yesterday. I saw you practice at the pool. Your diving is superb. No wonder you weren't on the swim team."

"I wasn't on any dive team, either," she said before she could stop herself.

"Why not?"

She shrugged, wishing she hadn't allowed the conversation to develop. "No time."

"With your kind of talent I would have thought you would have made time."

She passed him the damp towel and pulled on her

robe. "Well, I didn't," she admitted irritably, recalling the coaches and even her parents' attempts to make her change her mind. She headed for the door to the lanai.

Rich dabbed at his face, too interested in her reply to bother with his wet state. Suddenly two and two made four. He followed her quickly. "You didn't want to be seen in a suit in front of a crowd."

Christiana turned so fast, she almost fell over him. "No, damn it, I didn't. I popped out like this at the age of twelve. Boys and girls at that wonderful stage of development are not kind. Fighting for my virtue when I barely understood the mating ritual is worse than terrible."

Rich studied her flushed face, beginning to see more with each passing moment. Wasn't he cut of the same fabric? Hadn't he decided that women were fun, but not to be taken seriously for almost the same reasons that she had withdrawn from any kind of public show. She wasn't inhibited or even repressed. She was in pain, suffering from a past and surviving the best way she knew in the present. "I'm sorry," he murmured, risking reaching out to her one more time. When his fingers lightly touched her arm, covered in the thin terry, he knew that he had gotten closer than she permitted most people. Feeling oddly as though he were on trial, where a false word or move would condemn him to some unnamed punishment, he wrapped his hand around her arm.

"You did nothing."

"That doesn't mean I can't care that you're hurting."

Christiana shivered at the soft words that pierced

the illusion of her own invulnerability. "Not any more I'm not," she denied vehemently.

Rich opened his mouth to argue, only to be interrupted by Pippa's voice.

"Swimming, Rich? In your clothes?"

Christiana shrugged out of Rich's hold as he glanced over her shoulder at Pippa. "I fell in," he admitted, knowing the comment would draw Pippa's fire and give Christiana a chance to retreat if she needed to.

Christiana shot him a quick look. Shared secrets lurked in his eyes. Instead of feeling threatened by all that she had betrayed, she was oddly reassured that her trust, impulsive though it had been, wasn't misplaced. "He was trying to help me out. My foot slipped and I ended up dunking him," she added, turning to Pippa.

Josh glanced at his friend, his dark eyes alight with laughter. "I know I work you hard, but you didn't have to get even this way."

Rich laughed as he draped the towel around his neck. "Well, if you don't want me down with pneumonia, you'd better find me some dry clothes or talk Elsa into doing her best with this mess."

"And you had better get dry as well," Pippa added to Christiana. "The men came in for a late lunch and I haven't eaten, either. Join us."

Christiana shook her head. "The twins will be awake soon."

"Elsa's niece will look in on them until we're done."

Christiana knew an immovable object when she saw one. Pippa was definitely up to something. "All right," she agreed, deciding that a long talk with her zany employer was next on the list as soon as the two of them had some time alone. She glanced at Rich, curious at the thoughtful look on his face as he studied Pippa. Then he turned to her, one brow raised.

"Come on, Rich. I'll find you some clothes," Josh said.

"It's a good thing we're the same size," Rich replied, his expression changing in an instant. As Christiana left the room with the two men, she wondered at the play-within-a-play feeling she had about the trio. She was still examining the situation as she stepped into a hot shower. She didn't hear the knock on her door nor Rich when he walked into her room, calling her name. The first inkling she had that she wasn't alone came when, wrapped in a towel, she padded into the bedroom to find him staring out her windows, his back to the door of the bath.

"What are you doing here?" she demanded, stopping short.

He didn't turn. "We need to talk."

She stared at his back, realizing suddenly that although he had invaded her privacy he was making no attempt to embarrass her. Moving to the closet she quickly pulled on a robe. "You can turn around now."

He rotated, folding his arms over his chest as he surveyed her damp body in the concealing folds of white terry cloth. "How good are you at avoiding complications?"

Her brows raised. "Such as?"

"Our respective employers have a rather interesting turn of mind. Although to be perfectly honest, Pippa in this case is the linchpin to the problem."

"Cryptic utterances have never appealed. Clear English, please."

"You and I are being set up."

She frowned. "For what?"

"Marriage."

She stared. Nothing in his expression suggested he was joking. His voice was smooth, so unruffled he could have been reciting the telephone book. "Between us?" she asked finally.

His lips twisted into a grim parody of a smile. "Do you see anyone else in this room? Believe me, I'm not kidding. And neither is Pippa. That woman is lethal even in small doses."

"Could you be just a little paranoid on the subject of marriage?"

"Probably. But you don't know Pippa's history." He waved her to a chair. "We don't have much time so I'll make it short and bitter."

Christiana sat. Marriage? To Rich? With her? As she listened to Rich compress Pippa's eccentric twist on matchmaking, she began to see just what he was saying. "What do you have in mind?" she questioned at the end of the tale. "I assume you do have a plan."

"I wish I did. Pippa invented the word challenge. Telling her we're on to her tricks will just make her more determined to put us together, and I don't think we want the awkwardness of that. Nor do I want to hurt her feelings by coming down hard on her. She and Josh are my best friends and they have been there through some times in my life when I needed friends. You could quit."

"If that's the best you can come up with, think again. I like this job. Besides, I don't run."

"It's only a thought. Don't bite my head off."

"Well, think of something else."

"How about going along with the game?"

"You're crazy! That's the very thing we're trying to avoid."

"Think, woman."

"Don't call me 'woman' in that tone."

He sighed, raking his fingers through his hair. "If we both know what we're getting into, it can't do any harm to go along with the plan. As far as I can tell, Pippa's helping does have limits. We pretend to like each other, go out, then it fizzles. End of story. No one hurt. No confrontations. You keep your job, I keep my freedom and my friends."

"Frankly, it sounds like putting out a forest fire with a blow torch," she summarized irritably.

"Then you think of a better idea."

She glared. He returned her look with interest. "All right, so I don't have one. Give me a second." She got to her feet and wandered to her closet, thinking. Rummaging through her clothes, she pulled out a pair of pleated slacks and oversize striped shirt in peach.

"Don't you have anything that fits?"

"Mind your own business," she returned smartly without looking at him. A second later she jumped as Rich reached past her, searching through the garments for something more suited to his taste.

"What are you doing?"

"I refuse to make up to a woman who is bent on pretending she isn't built like a goddess. I'm not asking you to flaunt yourself like a vamp, but will you at least put on something that doesn't resemble a cut-up king-size sheet." He yanked a small plaid shirt from the last hanger he touched. "How did this get in here? It's actually your size."

Christiana snatched the blouse out of his hands, too angry to be polite. "I'll wear what I damn well please."

He smiled faintly, paying no attention to her temper. "Do you know your eyes spark when your world gets shaken up?"

"And you sound like a line out of a grade B movie."

"Do I? Maybe I ought to act like it, too."

Christiana had time for one outraged oath before Rich pulled her against his chest, trapping her arms between them. "You do this and so help me, I'll . . ."

Whatever she would have done was lost in the warmth of his mouth on hers. Her breath dammed in her throat as she struggled against his strength. No amount of wiggling gained her freedom. Needing air, she opened her lips. As if it were the signal he had been waiting for, Rich deepened the kiss. Christiana froze, stunned at the impact of the invasion. Her flailing ceased as waves of heat and emotion washed the anger from her mind. Passion, a past thought, suddenly became a reality too fantastic to fight. Her body softened, instinct taking over for inexperience. Her hands smoothed over his chest, the disputed blouse no longer held like a flimsy shield. Her moan of pleasure startled them both. Rich lifted his head slowly, staring into her eyes.

Christiana looked at him dazedly. "That was a mistake," she said huskily.

He touched her face, tracing the curve of her jaw down her throat to the hollow where her pulse raced for him. "Yes," he murmured absently. "It wasn't supposed to feel like that."

What sanity Christiana had left demanded she move away. But staying felt so much better. "It's only a kiss."

"It felt like an earthquake." He bent his head and touched her lips gently this time, lingering lightly over the lush surface. "Let's try it again and see what happens."

"You're crazy."

"You said that before." His mouth covered hers, learning her slowly, striving to please her with the simple caress. Her body felt right against his, but he was in no hurry to claim his prize. Waiting, going slow, seemed more important. His past had taught him the value of patience.

Christiana gave herself up to the kiss, needing this moment as she had few others in her life. His hands were sure on her body, supporting but not taking what she was not yet prepared to give. This time when he lifted his head, her breath was soft, rapid in the silence. "Definitely crazy," she whispered.

"Then we're crazy together," he whispered back, a challenge in his tawny eyes.

"What about our plan?"

"This makes it easier."

"Easier for one of us to get hurt."

"Life is like that." He kissed the corner of her mouth. "Come out and play, pretty diver. I promise not to jump you in a dark corner."

"What about lighted ones?" she grumbled, knowing, ill advised though it was, she would join Rich in this marriage plot.

"You can't have it all your own way," he pointed

out before setting her from him and taking the bulky blouse out of her hands, leaving the slimmer version behind. "Now dress before Pippa comes up to see what we're up to."

Christiana sent a theatrically hunted glance to the door.

Rich laughed.

"Turn your back," she commanded, chuckling with him.

"Spoilsport," he muttered, obeying. "I'll just envision you in that swimsuit. That ought to put me in the right mood to go downstairs."

"I have a feeling your plan is going to get us into more hot water than either of us wants." She yanked on her slacks, glaring at her image in the mirror. She looked fat. Snatching off the slacks, she jammed her hand in the closet and hauled out a pair of well-washed jeans.

"What are you doing? It can't take that long to put on your underwear and blouse and pants."

"Leave my underwear out of the conversation."

"You leave it off and I will."

Christiana stuck her tongue out at her new image before picking up a pillow and throwing it at Rich's back. He turned, clearly intending to retaliate. The arrested look on his face made Christiana look down at herself.

"You wear any more of those tents and I'll rip them right off that gorgeous body," he said, coming to her.

Christiana looked him straight in the eye. While she was willing to agree her need for camouflage had taken her to extremes, she wasn't prepared to allow him that kind of power. "You do and I'll blacken your eye."

He laughed. "I wouldn't let you."

She thought of her training and smiled sweetly. "Just try it and we'll see who will let whom do what."

He shook his head, liking her courage and the fire in her eyes even if he didn't believe she would or could take him on. "Let's have lunch. One of us needs food."

FIVE

Christiana watched Lori get out of her bath, wrapping a warm towel around the slippery, giggling little girl.

"I'm glad to see I'm not the only one who ends up looking as if I've has come through a tidal wave when I'm bathing these two," Pippa observed from the open bathroom doorway. J. Jr. stood at his mother's side, looking tidy, a feat in itself, in fresh pajamas, ready for his time with his parents as soon as his father got home.

"There are neater ways to give them their baths, but I like to see children splashing and playing," Christiana said, smiling down at Lori. "Your two are kind of special." She pretended not to see J. Jr.'s grimace at the description. The sturdy little boy had already begun to show the independence of mind and spirit that marked his mother and father.

Pippa's face reflected her maternal pride. "I think so, too, but I'm definitely prejudiced."

Christiana lifted Lori to her shoulder and moved into the bedroom. If J. Jr. had all the adventurous energy, Lori had the need for cuddling and loving.

"Sing to us," Lori commanded, her eyes pleading.

Christiana smiled, settling into one of the rockers by the window. Pippa took the other without a word. "What kind of song?"

"Something pretty."

"Yuck," J. Jr. mumbled from his place at his mother's side.

Lori glared at him. "Poke your fingers in your ears," she said irritably.

"One song," the little boy returned, leaning more heavily into his mother's lap.

Christiana began to hum, her voice soft and light. Pippa studied her, listening with the same rapt attention as her children. Like the twins, she found the sound soothing. As she watched the younger woman with her daughter, she was prey to a host of questions, none of which had she any intention of asking. The progress between Rich and Christiana was more than she had hoped for at this stage. After all it was only day three of her plan. She smiled faintly, suddenly lifting her head. Although the house was silent, she knew Josh had come home. She could feel his presence without seeing him. Her eyes focused on the door and in a minute he was there, his gaze locking with hers as though there were no one else in the room. Christiana stopped singing and rose. Without a word she handed the sleepy Lori to her father and left.

She entered her bedroom and debated going out for the evening. While she knew that she would be welcome at the table with Josh and Pippa, she had a sudden urge to give them their privacy. And she needed to be away from the epitome of all that she had wished for herself. The phone rang, startling her out of her melancholy thoughts.

"Tell me I'm not calling at a bad time."

Christiana sat down, honest enough to admit to herself she had hoped Rich would contact her. She couldn't forget those moments in the pool or the time after. He had made her feel so special, so womanly. The passion he seemed to command at will was addictive. She wanted more. For the first time in her life, caution and logic lost the battle with pleasure and challenge.

"You aren't," she answered huskily, the shades of emotion that he had unlocked inside her coloring her voice.

Rich heard the richness of her reply, finding it in a measure of his own need for reassurance. He had promised himself he wouldn't push, but he also knew he couldn't wait for the next chance meeting. He wanted to see Christiana, explore the strange attraction and affinity he seemed to have for this complex woman. "Good. Now tell me you are feeling as restless as I am and are interested in doing something—anything—tonight."

She smiled. The edge in his voice so closely resembled her own feelings of being off balance that she found herself relaxing slightly. "I am."

Rich hesitated, having expected her wariness to return in full force with the passing of a day. "You are?"

"Don't sound so stunned. I might take it as an insult."

"Don't." He was quick to reassure her. "I would really like to be with you. Dinner or whatever."

"All right. When?"

"Seven? Damn. That only gives you an hour. Make it seven-thirty. Or eight."

Laughing, she stopped him from adding another thirty minutes. "Seven is fine. An hour is plenty of time."

Rich frowned, visions of tents and sheets doing a fertility dance in his head. Once any of the two reached her closet he had no doubt they multiplied like rabbits. "Will I have to search through a mile of fabric to find you?" he asked bluntly.

"I do have something I would love to wear," she admitted, teasing him a little.

"Am I going to like it?" he demanded, suddenly suspicious of her tone.

"I'll let you decide," she murmured before gently hanging up the phone.

Rich listened to the dial tone thinking of what he was hoping for the evening and the reality of what would happen. Everything about Christiana told of a fastidious nature, a sensitivity and vulnerability. He couldn't think of a woman of his acquaintance even remotely like her. He also couldn't think of a time in his life when being with a woman hadn't been so easy that the words and actions came almost by rote. With Christiana he had to think every minute. Her wariness was both a challenge and a warning. He rose, stripping out of his suit, shirt, and tie, thinking of the night ahead. Desire was a rumbling demand for appeasement that he knew wouldn't be forthcoming. Yet, even that didn't matter. For the first time in a long while he was going out with a woman to simply enjoy being with her, to touch her mind, to share her laughter, and to watch the trust grow in her eyes. The needs of his body would wait this time. He didn't know how it had happened, but Christiana's wishes and feelings mattered more than his own. Quite simply, he wanted her to like him enough to drop her barriers and let him into her life. Even as he acknowledged the truth of his reaction to Christiana, he realized the cost to himself.

"I've got to be out of my mind," he muttered as he stepped, naked, into the shower. The water sluiced over his body, adding a sheen to taut muscles and long limbs. "There is no reason on earth why I should set myself up for a case of sleep-stealing frustration. I'm not a damn masochist," he added as he plunged his head under the shower and turned the taps to cold. Even as the water poured over him, Christiana's image danced in his mind. Anatomically he should have felt the cold enough to lose all interest. His oath when he found the age-old trick wasn't working was short and to the point. An interesting beginning for an evening supposed to be intended for enjoyment, he thought as he shot out of the cold shower and dried off briskly.

"Christiana is right. I am definitely crazy," he added for good measure.

Christiana stared at her reflection, frowning at the curves so faithfully displayed by the slim swath of butter-cream silk. The lines of the dress were elegantly simple—sleeveless, scoop neck curling gently around the tops of her breasts, and a soft swish of fabric to cling and slide over her hips to cup her buttocks. The hem flirted daintily with her knees. In short, an ordinary dress from the front. But the back was a different matter, and the cause of the frown that was not improving with the minutes spent in front of the mirror. The designer had gathered all the fabric up from hem to bodice so that material looped across her back leaving it bare all the way to the base of her spine. Only the clever cut and the creator's genius in the form of three thin straps, one across the base of her neck and the other two from the top of her shoulder to under her arm, kept the garment in place.

"I can't wear it," she mumbled. "I have to be out of my mind." She turned from her reflection, glaring at the dresses hanging in the open closet. "But I can't wear *them*, either," she all but wailed to herself. For the first time in her life she wanted a man to think her pretty . . . desirable.

"But not half naked," she muttered.

A short knock at her door shot a swift look of panic into her eyes.

"May I come in?" Pippa called.

Sighing, Christiana tried to relax. "Yes, of course."

Pippa entered, expecting to see a sample of Christiana's concealing wardrobe. She stopped short in surprise. "That's gorgeous. And perfect for your coloring," she said honestly, a delighted smile curving her lips. "You're beautiful."

Christiana shook her head even as the compliment brought a soft flush to her cheeks. "I think you've been writing fiction too long."

Laughing, Pippa plopped down on Christiana's bed. The silver tissue one-shoulder dress she was wearing embraced her body with almost as much ardency as Josh had less than an hour before. "Eye of the beholder," she replied, her eyes sparkling. "Wait until Rich sees you."

"Are you sure you don't mind my going out tonight?"

Pippa shook her head. "I told you the first day that your nights were your own unless Josh or I had an engagement. There are four adults here. We can manage, I promise." Her expression was kind, but her tone brooked no protest. "Now, you had better finish getting ready. Rich is one of the most punctual men I—"

At that moment, Christiana turned so that Pippa got her first look at the back of the dress. For one second, Pippa's expression blanked, then suddenly she was smiling a blindingly wicked smile that even Josh would have noted with deep misgiving.

"I do like your style," she murmured.

Christiana sat down with a groan. "I don't know why I bought it. I really don't. My only defense is the little shop where I found it had no mirrors to speak of. I needed something for a wedding and this felt so light, easy to wear, like I was wearing nothing, that I just took a chance."

"Well, you almost *are* wearing nothing, from the rear anyway," Pippa agreed, giggling. "Just as a matter of interest, what did the people at the wedding think of it?"

Appalled, Christiana stared at her. "I didn't wear it, of course. Once I tried it on at home I knew how unsuitable it was."

Before Pippa could comment, a thud at the door— Elsa's personal way of announcing her arrival—drew both women's attention. "Rich is here," she called through the panel before marching away.

"I can't wear this."

"Sure you can." Pippa got to her feet, showing a great deal of leg in the process. "It's a perfectly respectable dress and there isn't a man alive who won't appreciate it."

"I look like a woman on the make."

"Mule tails." Pippa grabbed Christiana's hands, yanked her to her feet, and pushed her onto the stool in front of the dressing table. "Do your face and remind yourself you have a spine and a brain. Rich has spent his life being a piece of meat on the wrong woman's plate. He knows what it's like to be stared at, to be judged as a body or a checkbook. He won't make that mistake with you."

"Why does it matter so much to you that we get together?" Christiana asked, watching her closely, wondering if Pippa would corroborate what Rich suspected.

Pippa hesitated, then shrugged. "Call it my writer's sight, or anything else you choose, but I am good at reading people. You aren't made to be an unsexed woman any more than Rich is destined to spend his life alone. And before you start thinking I'm trying to push you into anything heavy with Rich, I'm not. I won't deny I did my best to bring you two together. But that's all I'm doing. The rest is up to you. Both of you. But ask yourself this. Why did you go from that," she nodded toward the open closet and its concealing dresses and blouses, "to that . . ." Her hand drew a graceful arc to encompass the gown, the subtly drawn makeup that Christiana had put on and the soft swirls of curls teasing her shoulders, "if you had not wanted him to see you?" Without waiting to see how Christiana took her words, Pippa left the room, closing the door gently behind her.

Christiana stared at the panel, lost in thought. So much of what Pippa said made sense. But she had been in her niche for so long that the idea of coming out of it was frightening and yet exciting. A delicate rose traced her cheekbones as her eyes filled with shards of emotions too long kept under wraps. Rich had challenged her to come out and play and until this moment she hadn't realized just how much she needed this kind of gauntlet tossed her way. All her life she had balanced her recklessness against the knowledge of the consequences of unplanned action. Tonight with this man she would plan nothing. She would feel everything of which she was capable. And she would allow pleasure to guide her on paths she had never taken. This was her night and Rich was the man she had chosen with whom to share it. She left the bedroom, no longer worried about the scantiness of her gown.

"You are looking rather elegant tonight, Rich," Pippa murmured, attempting to read his expression. She should have known better than to try. Rich at his best gave rocks lessons on silence, both visual and verbal.

Rich smiled faintly, recognizing the probe and deflecting it easily. He hadn't expected to find amusement in Pippa's strange hobby. Tonight it was easy. "We're trying that new restaurant," he said blandly.

"And?"

"And what?" Rich asked, taking a sip from his drink.

Pippa sighed as she glanced at Josh. "I don't know why you haven't fired him by now. I ask a simple question and you'd think I was trying to pry company secrets out of him."

Josh chuckled. "You were being nosy," he pointed out unsympathetically, knowing exactly what was going through Pippa's mind. His look reminded her of their wager.

Before Pippa could find a discreet way to retaliate, she was thwarted by Christiana's entrance.

Rich rose, his eyes sliding over the simple dress. Every male instinct he possessed went on alert. Six cold showers wouldn't have stopped his response to the promise of her sleek body. His gaze lifted to hers. In those clear eyes he read the same anticipation that turned his blood to fire. He inhaled slowly before downing the last of his drink with one swallow.

Christiana looked away from his face, fighting the need to step into his arms and feel his warmth wrap around her. She had chosen this course, but she hadn't expected to be walking straight into flames the moment she saw him again. "Sorry I'm late," she said softly, surprised at the huskiness of her voice.

"It was worth the wait," Rich replied, setting down his glass. "We'd better go if we don't want to be late for our reservations." He came to her side, fighting the urge to kiss her right there in front of his friends and anyone else who cared to look.

Christiana read his intent as she fought her own skirmishes against the sensations splintering through her. When he took her hand, she gave it willingly. His smile at his own vulnerability invited hers. They made their good-byes quickly. As Christiana turned to precede Rich into the hall, he got his first look at her back.

"Where in the hell is the rest of this dress?" he demanded in shock. He stared at the expanse of bare flesh, watching as the muscles beneath the satiny flesh rippled with her every movement. The need to sling his jacket over her shoulders was fierce. What did she have on under it anyway? From the way it clung, dipped, and moved, it had to be precious little.

Christiana whirled around, her brows arching at the unexpected bite of his question. It hadn't occurred to her that he wouldn't like it. "You said you didn't like my other things."

"I don't, but I damn well didn't suggest something like this."

Neither noticed that Josh and Pippa, deciding it was a private discussion, edged past them to go upstairs.

Christiana glared. "I'm wearing this."

Rich didn't even notice the look or the way her breasts rose and fell with every agitated breath. He was too intent on the sudden change in her. "You can't."

She stared at him, unable to believe what she was hearing. "What do you mean, I can't?" Christiana was a calm woman, not given to tantrums, but she did have a temper. Although it took a lot to ignite it, once aflame it had the power to make Satan wish hell was deeper than China.

Rich fumbled for an explanation. "You hate men

looking at you. That damn dress is an open invitation to be ogled by the worst of them.''

"This dress is in perfect taste.'' The words were so soft that Rich had to bend to hear them.

"Maybe for someone like Pippa who makes a habit of this kind of thing, but not for you.'' The moment the words left his mouth, Rich knew he had made a serious tactical error in gaining Christiana's trust.

Christiana drew herself up, her breasts heaving beneath the thin cover. This time Rich didn't miss the show, almost swallowing his tongue in the process. Christiana's smile was dangerous. "I have changed my mind about going out with you.''

"Oh, no, you don't.'' Had Rich been thinking clearly he would have realized he had made enough stupid mistakes for one evening. He would have retreated in the best order possible and attempted to set things right after they both had calmed down. Unfortunately, his temper was more volatile than Christiana's and his frustration with emotions he hadn't expected made intelligence a dream. "We have a date and I have reservations.'' He reached for her hand.

Christiana tried to step out of range. The high heels that she had bought for the dress, the ones taller than those she was accustomed to, slid on the highly waxed floor. Rich grabbed for her as she started to fall. Her legs tangled with his. He overbalanced and they both landed with a thud, her groans and his curses mixing together.

Christiana pushed her arms against Rich's chest. Somehow he had managed to twist so that she had come down on top of him instead of crushed beneath him on the unforgiving hardness of the floor. Despite his care, her hair hung in her eyes and she could feel a definite draft around her hips. Her skirt felt as though it were a belt around her waist. "Let me up, you clumsy rat," she muttered, wiggling around, trying to untangle herself from him.

"So help me, woman, if you don't stop teasing me, I'm going to embarrass us both right in the middle of the foyer," Rich growled, trying to remember he was a grown man fully in control of his body.

At that second, Christiana felt the sharp nudge of thoroughly aroused male. She froze in midwiggle, staring down at him with wide, stunned eyes. "You can't be serious," she gasped.

"Does it feel as if I'm kidding?" he demanded furiously, never having been at such a disadvantage in his life.

"Don't shout at me."

Rich mentally cursed his position and the feel of this woman's body pressed intimately against his. His hands curled around Christiana's waist as he glared up at her. The shocked look in her eyes stilled the oath hovering on the tip of his tongue. She wasn't young. She had to know what she was doing to him and yet she looked as if she had never felt a man under her before. "How old are you?" he muttered, studying her expression, uneasy with the impossible idea sliding into his mind.

"Thirty-one."

"You act like you have never been in this position before. Why?" If he had been thinking clearly, he would have phrased his question with more tact.

Christiana felt the blush steal under her fair skin,

a dead giveaway to the answer she didn't have the courage to say.

Rich tensed, incredulity chasing the anger from his eyes. "You can't be serious."

She tried to bluff him with a haughty look. She might as well have saved herself the trouble.

"You're a virgin." It was completely impossible that no man had breached her defenses. He couldn't believe his entire sex was so stupid and inept. His gaze roamed over the unclaimed feminine territory lying so close to his heart and body. Suddenly he felt such a sense of responsibility, power that made leaping the moon seemed possible. The fact that Christiana had trusted him even a little took on more significance.

"Don't say a word," she hissed, anger and embarrassment adding edges to her usually soft voice.

He touched her face, his voice softening unconsciously. Her anger slipped through his thoughts without lingering. The need for answers had never been stronger. "Why? Have you been in a convent or something for most of your adult life? I know you've had a rough deal, but there must have been some man around with half a brain and eyes enough to look at your face, care about the person you are."

"Will you shut up?" she snapped, no longer caring if she wiggled or not. There was no way she was going to allow him to probe into this part of her life. Pushing her hands between them, she tried to lever herself erect.

Rich was having none of it. He tucked her close, ignoring her struggles. "Answer me. Why?"

"I will not," she panted, fighting harder for her freedom. "Let me up before someone sees us."

"No one can. When we slipped, your legs and mine slid into the salon. The only part of us that can be seen from the stairs or the hall is our heads. Besides, Josh and Pippa have already come out onto the landing, seen us lying here, decided we aren't dead, and retreated to their room. So has Elsa, or at least that thumping I heard sounded like her walk."

With his words the fight went out of Christiana. "They saw us?"

He nodded, still watching her eyes, trying to read the emotions chasing like summer lightning across the turbulent brightness. "Just the upper part, nothing else. I promise."

Christiana searched his face, seeing that he realized how little modesty she had left in their position. Once again the compassion in his gaze doused her temper. Her lashes dropped, giving her a visual isolation but no relief from the feel of his body, the strength of his hands holding her, and the warmth wrapping around her like a favorite guilt. "I didn't hear them," she admitted.

Rich lifted his other hand to her face, framing the slender bones that gave her features such character and purity. He watched her eyes open, finding untold messages in the cloudy depths. Gentleness was a new feeling for him. Desire, wanting, and needing he understood. The urge to protect and shelter was alien. "Don't be afraid of me."

Drawn by the slow, deep tone of his voice and the hidden meaning in the words, Christiana softened still more. "My experiences aren't good. I got tired of fighting for my virtue. Then you came, making me want things I thought I would never have," she confessed, unaware of the ease with which she told

him of her fears. Truth seemed more important than
hiding the past. If he cared about her at all he would
understand what she was saying. If he walked away,
then she would handle it. If he stayed, she would
know the trust that was beginning to grow was right,
good.

He stroked the hair back from her face, smiling
faintly. "You do the same to me. I had promised
myself that no woman would ever have any power
over me again. That I would be doing the taking
from now on. I don't feel that way with you," he
said quietly, her honesty demanding his in return. "I
want you more in this second than I have ever
wanted a woman in my life. But I'm not grabbing.
I'm not taking what you aren't ready to give."

"No, you're not," she agreed huskily.

Exerting only the lightest of pressure, he brought
her head down so that their lips were a mere breath
apart. Her scent was tantalizing every sense, but he
ignored the lure to concentrate on the whole woman.
"I would very much like a kiss."

Christiana looked at his mouth, wanting that kiss
and the man who cared enough to ask. "You
would?" she whispered.

He nipped gently at her lower lip. "I would. Your
mouth is as gorgeous as the rest of you. I want to
taste it again." Then the top lip knew the bite of his
need. "Say yes." He remembered their first kiss
well. He had given it to the woman he had thought
her to be, gentle, hurt, but experienced. She had
responded, but it had been more of temper and surprise than passion slowly and carefully nurtured. This
time he wanted her to feel the birth of what could

lie between them. He wanted her wholehearted participation.

"Yes."

His lips settled lightly on hers, moving slowly across the full contours, learning her and giving her a chance to learn him. When she sighed softly, he deepened the kiss, letting her feel the tip of his tongue. In a moment her lips parted.

Christiana gave herself up temporarily to the experience of being handled as she had always hoped for but never actually known. She hadn't known a man could give so completely. Fire built slowly, her muscles going fluid with the heat. When he pulled his mouth from hers, she actually felt regret and loss. Her eyes opened as she stared into his. His smile was hers.

"Did you like that?"

"Yes."

His questions were so simple, answering was easy.

Rich released her face, sliding his hands down her body. "Lift up a little, pretty diver."

Christiana obeyed, still watching the changing expressions on his face. A second later, she realized that he was pulling her dress down until she was decently covered. "Why?"

"I'm not the peeping Tom type. If and when I see the rest of this glorious body, it won't be because you're embarrassed or at a disadvantage." He traced the length of her nose with the tip of his finger. "I like you. I want you to like me."

"You make it sound so uncomplicated."

"It is." He grinned. "Of course, if you'd like to drop that dress off sometime where we have privacy and about ten years to indulge my fantasies, I won't fight you at all.''

Christiana laughed, her amusement as uninhibited as her response to his kiss had been. ''You mean you aren't going to start yelling about it again.''

Rich pushed himself into a sitting position, tumbling her into his lap before she could realize his intentions. He cradled her in his arms, smiling into her startled eyes. ''Let's put it this way. You can wear the dress as long as I'm along to protect your virtue.''

''That sounds like something out of a Victorian novel.''

''Honey, it also sounds like one territorial male. Me.'' He bent his head, kissing her swiftly before setting her away from him. ''Let's get out of here before we miss dinner and I forget my good intentions.''

''Do you have any?'' she asked as she got to her feet. This time she treated the waxed floor with the respect it deserved.

Rich took her arm as an added precaution. ''I'll let you decide.''

SIX

The bar was dark, noisy, and in a part of town few respectable people knowingly frequented. The figure slipped among the tables, something about the walk and the way the eyes stared through the crowd silencing those it passed and creating an aura of stealth and menace. A back booth was its destination and the two men lounging there whom it had come to see.

"Well?" a voice demanded gruffly, indistinguishable in terms of gender or age.

The smaller of the pair shifted uncomfortably. This job, despite its simplicity, was making him nervous. He didn't like the boss.

"We did what you told us," the taller one answered defiantly, glaring up into a face that he couldn't have described well even if interrogated.

"Like hell. If you had, the formula would be ours now. Instead we've got a bird dog. Martin Richland. I want him out and don't blow it this time." The

91

figure tossed a slip of paper toward the speaker. "He'll be at this restaurant tonight. Take him out."

"Hey, wait a minute," the shorter man objected. The minute those dead eyes turned in his direction he wished he had kept his mouth shut.

"Yes."

The single word was a chill of ice down his spine, but Rollo lived in a jungle where to show fear was a warrant for his own death. Swallowing the bile that rose in his throat, he pushed out his protest. "You can't mean murder. We told you, we don't do that kind of stuff."

"You said you'd take care of your mistakes. You blew it and now Richland is on our tail. Your fault. Not mine." Every word was a verbal bullet.

"But how?" Dingo, the taller, asked.

"I don't care. Just make no mistakes or I'll find someone else who wants fifty grand." Without another word the figure rose and glided out the door and into the night.

"Pippa, I should wring your beautiful neck. Christiana is not the type of woman to wear your style of clothes. I would have bet my money on your perception. Why did you do it?"

Pippa wound her arms around Josh's neck, ignoring his confused scowl. "I didn't do it, my love. She picked that little number out all by herself."

"I don't believe it," he said flatly. "That woman wears enough material between her and the outside world to carpet this house."

"She has her reasons."

"And I'm not so insensitive I can't guess at them. But what about Rich?"

"He'll handle Christiana and she'll take care of him. Trust me."

Josh pulled his wife close, looking into the pale-blue eyes that seemed to hold the knowledge of the universe. "They don't look very well matched to me."

"Neither did we, and look how that turned out."

"You pregnant at forty-two and me a father at my age."

She laughed huskily, beginning a slow, teasing wiggle against him. "And you love it."

"I love *you*," he corrected roughly, hauling her against his chest and off her feet. "Damn, you're dynamite and I'm the fuse. When I'm ninety I'll still be chasing you."

"Don't worry, my love, I'll make sure you have the faster wheelchair."

"Well, what do you think of this place?" Rich asked, leaning back in his chair as he watched Christiana. The waiter had just departed with their orders. Music provided by a live harpist played softly in the background. Cypress paneling and ceiling fans lent a touch of the tropics while the handsome carved cages of finch and love birds offered an interesting but soothing focal point for the decor.

Christiana glanced around, then back at him. Rich made conversation easy. Because he knew her background, because he had shown her respect as a person, she felt no pressure to perform as a date. The look in those tawny eyes spoke of admiration, but there was no demand in his gaze or his touch, only a wish to please and be pleased. "It's fascinating. How did you hear about it?"

"One of the secretaries at the office recommended it."

Christiana lifted her glass, sipping the cool white wine she had ordered. Smiling, she added, "I applaud your taste and hers."

Rich returned the gesture, liking the way she flirted so gently. Aggressive women had never appealed to him and yet the world seemed populated with that species. With every second in Christiana's company he realized how unique she really was and how intrigued he was becoming with her. "Tell me about yourself."

"Specifically?" One brow raised curiously at the sudden depth in his voice.

"Anything. Everything. Like how you came to be untouched."

If something in Rich's expression hadn't warned her he was about to be outrageous, Christiana knew she would have disgraced both of them by choking on her wine. "I already told you," she whispered, glancing frantically around to see if anyone had heard. The seclusion of their table, plus the lush greenery that was placed at strategic intervals to provide privacy for each seating, reassured her.

Rich reached across the table and took her hand. "I'd rather know the whole story than make educated, though possibly wrong, guesses. Won't you trust me?"

"I do, a little more every time I see you. But you're going too fast," she admitted honestly.

He sighed but didn't release her. "But don't you see. Unless I know the worst, I'm stumbling around in the dark. I don't want to blunder into hurting you."

"Perhaps there won't be any stumbling," she returned, feeling cornered and not liking the sensation.

His lips lifted in a slow smile. "Your memory is sure a lot shorter than mine."

Christiana damned her fair skin as she felt the heat creep over her cheeks.

"Lord, that blush is pretty," Rich murmured, watching her. "I don't think I've ever known a woman who could do that."

"I don't see why not. You have a way of slicing through discretion and tact," she replied smartly, holding her own. Her body might be virgin territory, but her mind was strictly today's female.

"Tact is only a tool, not a state of thought. You interest me."

"My body interests you," she corrected, for one moment allowing the lessons of the past to overshadow what she was learning in the present. "And the fact that no one has had it before you and that I was fool enough to let you see that I find you attractive."

Rich bit down on the anger threatening to boil over at her words. Understanding where they came from hadn't given him any armor against their slice.

Christiana winced as his fingers closed tight on her hand. "You're hurting me. Let me go," she commanded, damning her tongue and the tear in the fabric of understanding her hasty words had made.

Rich loosened his grip but didn't release her completely. His eyes held hers. "Do you really believe that?" he demanded roughly, incensed by her cynicism and the faint truth of his actions. He couldn't deny his body did want hers. And that he was more glad that he wouldn't have admitted out loud that he would be the first man in her life. But damn it, that wasn't all there was to the attraction.

The past demanded she say yes. But the memory of his gentleness, his compassion, froze out the word. "No."

"I could handle it better if you had been experienced. I don't know how to act with you. I'm having to learn as I go. I don't like being off balance." The sentences were sharp lances of honesty from a man who had learned the value of evasion.

Caution raised its head. "Then walk away."

"I'm no coward. Just because this is new to me, awkward, doesn't mean I'm running."

"Neither am I," Christiana retorted, stung.

"Then don't bring it up as an alternative."

"I don't want a lover."

At that moment the waiter appeared with their appetizers. Christiana snatched her hand from Rich's, wishing one of those lush potted palms was close enough for her to hide under. The smile on the man's lips and the openly appreciative look he gave her didn't help at all. In her embarrassment, she missed Rich's lethal glare and the sudden discretion of the younger man in the quick way he served them and melted away.

"He's gone," Rich murmured, watching her.

Christiana shrugged, trying to look as though it didn't matter. "You must think I have a lot of hang-ups."

"Not hang-ups. Defenses. I've got them, too. A woman mentions marriage and I start backing up, literally. I've been down the aisle three times and every trip was worse than the one before."

Forgetting herself for a moment, Christiana leaned

forward to pick up her fork and start on the mushrooms in hollandaise sauce she had ordered. "Why did you try it that many times?"

"I wanted something very simple. A family. My parents didn't have one and I spent most of my life trying to find some kind of security that didn't have a dollar sign attached. I wanted someone to share with, someone who truly cared how I felt, what I thought. I wanted to be able to give those things in return. Unfortunately, I guess I was so accustomed to the kind of relationships that I had always known that I just didn't have the ability or judgment to create something different with the women I have chosen."

Without thinking, Christiana reached across the table to touch his hand. "It was their loss." The cynical way he met her eyes hurt. She drew back, unaware that his look was a mirror of her own when she was facing her past.

"Platitudes?" His brows rose, skepticism in his voice.

"Truth. The same commodity you offered me. Don't you recognize it?"

"The lady has a sting in her tail."

"The lady has a fork in her hand," Christiana corrected meaningfully.

He inclined his head, amused at her and a little irritated at himself. He had meant to show her the similarities between them, and at the first sign of interest on her part he had pushed her away. "So you do," he drawled, determined to stop reacting to things that no longer should have the power to hurt him. "But I don't intend to give you a reason to use it on me. In fact, I'll apologize."

Christiana didn't trust the probing look in his eyes. "For what?"

"I don't usually slap away a hand meant to soothe. I have so little of that in my life."

The words sounded sincere enough, but the delivery was almost too smooth. Wary, Christiana asked, "What do you want from me?"

"You've already asked me that."

"And?"

"I told you. I want to get to know you."

"Biblically?"

"I wouldn't object and, if you're honest, I don't think you would, either."

"But no marriage, no commitment?"

"I don't grab and you don't trap. I would have thought it a fair exchange."

"Sounds like an affair to me."

"Would that be so bad?"

"It's going to sound crazy, but I don't know. For the first time in my life, I'm confused," she said slowly, her expression bewildered. "I've tried to be logical, but it doesn't work." Her smile was slight, a little sad, very wise. "For the first time in my life, my body won't listen to my brain. Maybe I do want an affair. Maybe you have the right of it. I know I'm lonely. I know that I can imagine myself in your bed all too easily. What I don't know is if I can really do it without regret."

Rich stared at her, shocked by the reply he hadn't expected. Confusion had never been his strong suit. This woman was nothing like any other. Here she was sitting primly in her chair in a dress that even Pippa wouldn't have worn, discussing having an affair with him over appetizers of mushrooms and oysters when a few moments before she had looked as if she wanted to hide because the waiter heard her say she didn't want a lover. Now there wasn't even a blush in evidence, he thought, feeling oddly cheated.

"You are one contrary female," he muttered, wondering if she had changed personalities when he wasn't watching.

Christiana's lips twitched, surprising her with the need to laugh. Whether it was at him or herself she didn't know and strangely cared even less. It was enough that she had disconcerted him. "I would hate to be predictable."

"Well, you are definitely not that," he agreed, stabbing an oyster. "I thought you would condemn the idea out of hand."

"A few days ago I would have. You are one very unsettling man, Martin Richland, III," she replied, digging into her mushrooms. If someone had told her that she would be discussing such intimate details over dinner on her first date with him she would have called that person a liar. But, as everything else with Rich, she was finding the usual was distinctly not on the agenda. The man was a rare find in a world filled with clones.

"This is nuts. You get the chair for this in Florida," Rollo grumbled as he stared at the entrance to the fancy restaurant that had been the address on the paper the boss had thrown at them.

"Will you just shut up?" Dingo demanded irritably. "I don't wanna do this any more than you do. But that guy in there worries me less than the boss."

"Yeah," Rollo agreed glumly. "Don't like rich dudes anyway. Bet he never had to work for anything

in his life." He shoved an elbow into Dingo's ribs.
"Look, there he is! Gawd, look at that woman with
him. Wow!"

"Keep your mind on the job," Dingo growled,
starting the car. "We mess this up and our tails are
in a sling for sure." He pulled out as the sports car
entered the flow of traffic. "Let's just hope our man
there takes his doll to his place for a little quickie."

Rollo shifted in his seat, his eyes glued to the
car they were following. "Don't look that way. They're
heading more for where that woman is supposed to
be staying."

Dingo swore. "Damn fool. Bet the SOB is gay or
something."

Traffic thinned out. Dingo dropped back to avoid
being spotted as he waited for a moment to implement his hastily drawn plans.

"I really enjoyed myself tonight," Christiana murmured, watching the easy way Rich handled the car.
Strangely enough she meant it, too. After they had
settled the course for the future, their meal had
turned into a easy flow of conversation and compan-
ionable silences that were soothing yet stimulating.
She had needed the strengthening of the mental and
emotional ties before she committed herself further.
She suspected Rich did as well.

"You're an easy passenger," he said, smiling at
her in the darkness.

He exited the interstate to a dark side road that
wound around the residential side of the river. The
houses here were few, large estates mostly with lots
of land between homes. In the daylight it was a pic-

turesque drive, and at night romantic when the moon was full as it was this evening.

"I'm glad you agreed to come out with me again."

She laughed softly. "If we are going to have an affair, I want to know more about you first."

"And I you," he said huskily, downshifting to make a sharp curve. Suddenly there was a jerk and then the uneven thuds of a blown tire. Rich got the car under control and edged to the narrow shoulder of the road. "Do you know, in all the years I've been driving, this is only the second time this has happened to me?"

The disgust in his voice touched Christiana's humor. "I thought men swore at a time like this."

"The thought had occurred, but it won't change the fool thing, so why bother," he pointed out, opening his car door. "At least I've got a moon to see by and someone to hold the flashlight."

Christiana opened her door and joined him on the side of the road. "You've got an interesting way of asking for help, Richland."

Rich pulled her close and kissed her before she could object. "Woman, didn't your mother ever teach you it isn't safe to tease a man having car trouble. We tend to need a target for our temper," he whispered against her lips.

Her eyes gleamed softly in the silver light of the moon. "And me without my fork."

"Keep that up and I'll think of better things to do with this deserted area and you."

"Promises, promises."

Rich looked at her lips and the smile lurking there and felt a kick of desire so intense that he almost forgot himself enough to grab for what was not yet his. This time he did swear as he set her from him. "Let's get this tire changed before I forget I'm supposed to be a gentleman."

Suddenly the sound of another car intruded in the silence.

Rich urged her as far off the tree-lined shoulder as possible. "That curve isn't going to make us very visible, and whoever that fool is, he's coming at too fast a clip. Better the car gets hit than us."

Christiana slipped into the line of trees, knowing the sense of his precaution. A second later the car pulled to a stop in a squeal of brakes behind theirs. She felt Rich tense as he watched two men get out.

Rich studied the pair, not liking the way they moved so furtively toward his vehicle. Suddenly the moonlight glinted off metal. Guns. "Go up into the trees, and if you see a chance to run, take off through the woods for that house we passed. It shouldn't be more than a mile away," he commanded without looking at Christiana. "Now! Get out of here."

Expecting Rich to follow, Christiana obeyed without taking her eyes from the pair inspecting the car. As yet neither had seen them as the shadows from the dense foliage had shielded them from view. Almost immediately, Christiana found herself surrounded and protected by the trees. She turned, looking for Rich. He wasn't there. She stared through the leaves barely able to make out the men who had stopped. But their voices carried clearly.

"They couldn't have gone far. That woman wasn't wearing shoes built for walking. In fact, I don't think they tried to walk." Dingo looked up the slight slope.

Christiana froze, knowing the slightest movement could give her hiding place away. He seemed to be looking straight at her even though she knew he couldn't possibly see her.

"You might as well come out now. Make it easier on yourselves, Richland. You can't hide the woman in that yellow dress, especially with this moon," Dingo called.

Christiana studied the speaker and the gun he held. Had she been a stranger to danger, the kind of menace the man projected would have had her quivering in fear. As it was, anger was her overriding emotion. While she didn't understand the reasons these people were after her and Rich, there was no doubt they intended harm, if not actually death, before the night was over. She could run, but that would mean turning her back to the enemy and leaving Rich with two-against-one odds and no weapon. Neither thought was palatable. She would not run. Her training and her inclination demanded she stay and face the threat.

The moment the gunman's eyes moved from her to search the area around her, she slipped carefully out of her shoes. The tight dress had to go as well. Without regret, she leaned down, took the hem at the side seam between her hands, and yanked strongly. The delicate fabric tore in one clean rip halfway up her leg. She repeated the process on the other side. She wished she knew what Rich's plan was. With neither of them armed, she suspected he would be more concerned with protecting her than himself. Now it was her turn to search the area, hoping for some sign of Rich.

A second later his voice sounded far away to her right. "What do you want?"

The two men reacted by moving toward him and away from her. Christiana's mind ticked over with possibilities as she listened to the night and the men who would rent the stillness with violence. Rich was drawing them away from her, a chivalrous move but one that put him in more danger for her. The price of her safety for his. The will to survive at any cost rose to mate with her anger, becoming a single, controlled force alive with energy and clear thought. Twice in her life she had been called on to use her training, both in situations as uneven as this one. She needed a weapon, preferably something she could throw. The open trunk should provide what she needed. A jack handle and a wrench if she were lucky. Edging carefully down the slope, she kept her eyes on the men. Neither seemed to care that she and Rich might have separated if they had even thought of the probability. She reached the back of the car without being detected. Crouching at the bumper, she felt in the trunk, her fingers touching cold metal. Breathing a prayer, she lifted first the jack handle from its storage place and then a small tool box.

"Might as well take a screwdriver as well as a wrench. It isn't a knife, but it will do in a pinch," she muttered, collecting her loot and sliding the box back into place.

"We want you and the pretty lady," Rollo answered.

Rich eyed the pair, hoping Christiana had sense enough to take off for help. He didn't know how long he could play hide-and-seek with the pair of armed thugs in this moonlight. Damn what he wouldn't give for a gun of his own.

SEVEN

Damning the pale-yellow dress that glowed like a neon sign in the moonlight, Christiana stole through the shadows, using every available inch of cover. She had a fairly good arm and an even better aim, but she wanted every foot she could to get closer to her targets. The voices of Rollo and Dingo carried easily as neither was making much of an attempt at secrecy.

"You circle left, Rollo," Dingo directed, waving his hand to indicate the small clump of trees in front of them.

Rollo obeyed, his gun making controlled, wide sweeps of the area.

Rich slid carefully backward, keeping his eyes on the men. He had chosen his hiding place well, anticipating just this kind of a maneuver. The rock in his hand wasn't as good as a gun but it was better than nothing. Now all he had to do was to get his stalkers separated. He didn't relish getting shot by one when he stood up to throw at the other.

Rich held his position, his eyes narrowed on the closest man. He could no longer see and could barely hear the other moving in the bushes to his right. Suddenly a faint flash of color behind Dingo caught Rich's eye. Yellow. Christiana. The words shouted in his mind, although no sound emerged to betray her. Damn and double damn. What was that crazy woman up to? Forgetting his plan, he eased down the hill as swiftly as possible. Didn't she realize the danger? She was only fifteen or so feet from Dingo. He watched her rise.

Swearing softly, he tossed a branch off to his left. Then he popped up himself, hoping the twin maneuvers would confuse the other man. His hand tight on the rock, he shouted, "Hey, Dingo."

Dingo swiveled to the left, firing from the silenced gun.

Seeing her chance, Christiana jumped out of the shadows and threw the wrench with a side-arm sling that caught Dingo at the base of his neck down to his shoulder blades. He hit the dirt as though every bone and muscle had turned to water. Before Dingo made contact with the ground, Rich was on his feet, running. A quick look assured Rich that Dingo was out for the count as he scooped up his weapon and tucked it in the small of his back. Turning, he crossed the few remaining feet in a silent rush to crouch down beside Christiana.

"Are you crazy, woman?" he hissed, fear for her and rage at the situation making his voice a lethal slice of sound.

"No, just mad as the devil," she hissed back, straining to catch a glimpse of Rollo. "I hope that creep has a headache the size of Europe when he wakes up. Where is his rotten friend? Do you see him?"

Rich stared at her, stunned at the deadly purpose in her tone. Far from being frightened and in need of protection, she looked ready to take on the other thug at the drop of a hat or in this case, he decided with a grim amusement, with a jack handle and a screw driver. "Give me one of those. I don't want to use the automatic unless I have to," he said tersely. "You knocked out Dingo. The least you could do is let me handle the other one. Think of my ego." The last he added with a touch of honest amusement. Now that they were together and safe, his anger no longer mattered.

Startled at the humor at a time like this, Christiana turned her head just in time to collect a rough kiss on her parted lips. "Are you nuts?" she demanded, feeling his need all the way to her toes.

His crooked grin flashed in the muted light. He should have known better than to expect the norm from a woman who had shown herself to be far from usual. "If I am, you are, too." He reached down and pulled the jack handle out of her hand.

Christiana opened her mouth to speak, but the sound of someone blundering through the woods stilled her words. "The villain cometh," she said instead.

"Little knowing that an Amazon and her mate lurk in the forest waiting in ambush."

She laughed softly, this time taking her own kiss with a fierce possessiveness. "Go get him, mate. I'll watch my victim."

Rich inclined his head, knowing she would do it,

too, doing whatever it took to protect herself and him.

Christiana kept her eyes on Dingo, acutely aware of Rich slipping into the trees. Minutes later she heard a thud and a broken-off cry of pain in almost the same instant. She tensed, her fingers tightening on the screwdriver just in case Rollo was the next person she saw.

"Two down and none to go," Rich announced, coming out of the shadows, dragging the unconscious Rollo by his collar. The deadly gun the other had carried was tucked in the waistband of Rich's slacks. "Now let's get this rat and his friend tied up and then we'll get help."

Christiana rose, the torn dress displaying a long length of leg. Rich stared at the damage, a scowl drowning the satisfaction of capture. "What happened to you?"

Christiana looked down at the mutilated gown without regret. "I ripped it. You try walking in this thing, much less skulking about in the bushes, dodging idiots waving guns," she returned smartly.

Rich chuckled at her disgusted tone as he stripped off his belt to wrap it around Dingo's hands. He had already parted with his tie to truss up the hapless Rollo. "You wouldn't have been skulking in the bushes if you had done what I told you."

"The last time I did what anyone told me, outside of my work that is, I was about eight. It was a male, too. He wanted me to climb a tree that had the lowest branch higher than he could reach. Since I was a good head taller, I had the dubious honor of going after his kite. I fell and broke my arm and the little brat denied all knowledge of why I had ignored the rules and been in the tree in the first place."

"Serves you right for listening to the kid," Rich pointed out unsympathetically.

"Just what I thought. And subsequent situations have hardened that decision into stone."

Rich gave the belt one last yank, then straightened to survey her calm face. He hadn't missed the way she had handled the firearm. "How about telling me who you are?"

"You know."

"Your name, maybe. What I don't know is why a nanny would know about makeshift weapons, violence, guns and skulking in the bushes. In short, where is the fear? You're too damn calm."

"You think tears and trembling little female shakes would have been better," she challenged him with a straight look.

"No. But it would have been understandable." He folded his arms, waiting.

There was no reason not to tell him. "I trained at a rather special school in England. With so many of the wealthy and the politically influential and their families at risk all over the world, there is a new niche needed in baby- and child-rearing. I and others like me are combination baby-sitters, nurses, and bodyguards. I can drive any vehicle. Make weapons out of sticks, strings, and rocks. Handle most guns, all bows and knives, although I'm not too thrilled with the last. Close work offers too many chances for me getting hurt. I swim and dive better than the average person. You already know that. Have a few certificates in first aid, rescue work, and CPR. I've climbed a mountain or two, for entertainment, not work." She spread her hands, smiling faintly at his stunned expression. "And have most of the social accomplishments, although those, like knives, aren't my favorite things. Oh, and I can ride a camel."

"Useful talent," he remarked dryly.

"It is in the desert. Especially if you want to find water. Nasty as he is, a camel will find something to fill his belly."

"I'm surprised Josh didn't mention that you had these kind of credentials."

"I don't think he knows. Pippa never asked, and it wasn't a job requirement." She shrugged, glancing down at Dingo as he groaned. "I think they're waking up."

Rich prodded one man with a foot. "Looks that way." Bending, he hauled the man upright and waited while the other scrambled drunkenly erect. "Walk." He urged them in the direction of the cars.

Dingo stumbled forward, almost pitching on his face. Rich caught him as Christiana followed close behind. "We'll get these two down to the cars. If you'll watch them while I change the tire, then you can go for help. That junker of theirs looks all right, but I would prefer not to take any chances at this point."

"We could stuff them in the trunk of their car. It should be big enough to hold them until the police arrive. We can't be more than three miles from Pippa's anyway."

Rich shook his head, his lips twitching. "Aren't you ever squeamish?"

She considered the idea. "No," she decided finally. "One of my mother's most often repeated comments was that I hadn't a gentle or romantic bone in my body. I don't cry. When I'm threatened I fight back and I don't quit.'' She couldn't even think why she was telling him all this. It had to be the night and the extraordinary demands that had been made on them. The situation had forged strong bonds of the camaraderie of war. And intimacy of sorts she should distrust and didn't.

"An Amazon."

"I've been called worse. Besides, it's apt with my size."

"Someday remind me to tell you what I think of Amazons."

"Whoever our enemy is, he or she isn't playing around with the small stuff. Murder in this state can get a death sentence," Pippa murmured, putting into words what everyone was thinking.

The police had just left after an hour of extensive questioning. Josh and Rich had outlined the situation they believed was the motivation behind the attempt to make sure Rich was out of action.

"What I don't like is that you didn't tell me what was going on, darling," Pippa continued, turning to her spouse.

Josh met her look with a raised brow and a shrug. "You had enough with the twins, trying to find someone to take care of them and still meet your deadline. Frankly, I didn't think the problem would bleed into my private life. I won't make that mistake again."

Pippa studied her husband, knowing he had taken the hint. Satisfied, she turned to the next of her targets, Christiana. "I would like to know why a woman with your qualifications would be working in this kind of a household? We must be tame stuff.''

Smiling faintly, Christiana shook her head. ''Tame is the last word I would use to describe this household.''

Pippa wasn't diverted. ''You know what I mean,'' she said with a determined gleam in her eye.

Christiana shrugged, aware that the moment she had revealed her background to the police with Pippa and Josh listening, she would face this question. Her answer was simple. ''I was tired of living abroad, hearing languages that weren't my own. I was in danger of forgetting who I was. I came home, or as near to home as possible. Marie allowed me to stay with her until I settled my life. Her agency doesn't have much call for my kind of job so I took what was available.''

''You could have worked in Washington or any major city,'' Pippa said, stating the obvious.

''Jacksonville seems large enough.''

''And, at the moment, dangerous enough to need your particular qualifications,'' Josh inserted bluntly. ''I, for one, don't care why you're here, as long as you can keep my children safe. If the person we're up against is desperate enough to make a murder attempt on Rich, and you by association, then none of us is safe.'' He looked at Pippa, knowing she wouldn't thank him for denying the knowledge he could already see in her eyes.

Pippa slipped her hand in his. ''Josh is right. Whatever your reasons, we're glad you're here for the twins.''

Christiana released a soft sigh of relief. She hadn't consciously lied about herself, but she had left a lot out and that had bothered her. Especially when Pippa had been so quick to call her friend. "I'll guard them with my life," she said simply.

Josh squeezed Pippa's fingers.

Reading the husbandly signal, Pippa rose. "I don't know about the rest of you, but I'm done in. I'm going to bed."

Christiana, too, had gotten the silent message that the men needed some time alone to discuss the situation. "I'll come with you." She glanced at Rich, not surprised to find him watching her. The tenderness mixed with admiration in his eyes was becoming something she looked for. The knowledge and the image stayed with her as she left Pippa outside her bedroom door and slipped into the darkness of her room to strip off her ruined dress.

Josh went to the bar to pour himself another drink. He returned to the couch, sighing heavily as he sat down. "What do you think?"

"I think that there must be even higher bidding going on for our project than we suspected," Rich said bluntly. "And someone in this mess thinks we're getting close to him or her." He took a restless turn around the room. He had retrieved his belt from Dingo's wrists. His shirt and slacks showed liberal traces of his passage in the woods. His hair was rumpled as though his hands had been thrust through it in anger, frustration, or both. His wrinkled, ruined tie hung like a scarf around his neck. "I just wish I knew what rock I turned up and missed the worm underneath."

"So do I. I don't like having my family or friends in danger."

"Neither do I." He threw himself in the chair, glaring at Josh without really seeing him. "When I was watching Christiana work her way behind that creep with the gun, I found out what helplessness feels like. When she took him out I didn't know whether to kiss her or wring her neck."

"I know the feeling."

Rich focused on Josh, a grim smile lighting his face momentarily. "Yeah, I guess you do."

"Get used to it. It isn't going to get any better."

"Don't make it sound so permanent. You better than anyone know I'm not into that anymore."

"Christiana could change your mind."

Rich's smile died swiftly. "No way. Three was bad enough."

"They hardly counted."

Again, Rich got to his feet. "Drop it. We have more important things to think about. Like how do we catch this guy? And where will he strike next?"

Josh studied his friend, knowing his suggestion was going to be as unpopular. "I've been thinking about that. As it stands right now, we have a mole of some kind in the organization. With the exception of the two of us, I don't trust anyone else. Without doing a room-to-room sweep at the office every morning, we can't even be sure that the area is bug free. On top of that, we're at risk every time we set foot outside these gates. I don't like any of this. And until we know the direction in which the danger lies, it is just you and me against an unnamed foe."

Rich made a move to interrupt. As yet, Josh had said nothing he hadn't already considered.

"I think you ought to move in here. There isn't enough security around your building, but there is here. We've got the guards. And we can be in close contact in an area where we don't have to worry about bugs.''

''The reason I live where I do is because there are no guards. I had enough of that growing up.''

Josh looked him straight in the eye. ''You can pander to your phobias any other time. Right now, work with me on the living arrangements, at least until we have some idea what we're dealing with.'' Josh leaned forward to put his empty glass on the table. The move was as tightly controlled as his anger. ''I want these people, but not at the cost of you, anyone I care about, or myself. I'm past the age where I believe in immortality.''

Startled at his wording, Rich stared at Josh, reading something more than the seriousness of the situation in his expression. ''What aren't you telling me?''

''Joe called.''

Rich knew and liked Joe but his psychic gift was not something with which he was either comfortable with or knowledgeable about. ''When?''

''Right after you and Christiana left.''

''And?''

''He felt the attack coming. He sees black without end around you.''

Rich turned the possibility over in his mind. ''Death?''

''He never uses that name because he doesn't believe in the concept of death as you and I know it.''

''Then what? Should I run because of this blackness? I'm not built that way and you know it.''

''Precautions. Only a fool wouldn't take them.''

''Would you?''

"Yes, without griping about it, too," he admitted with a sigh. "Besides, look on it as a chance to see more of Christiana."

"She might not want to see more of me."

Josh's disbelieving look spawned Rich's glare. "I may not have Pippa's hand at matching, but that woman is definitely interested, and so are you."

"Bribery?"

He shrugged, ignoring the caustic tone. "Whatever works."

Rich released his breath with a rough oath. Josh's plan made sense even if it did go against the grain. "All right. But I think this is overkill."

"Just so long as it isn't human kill."

EIGHT

Rich grunted irritably, rolling over in the strange bed to glare at the bright moon that insisted on sitting right outside his window. Sleep was impossible. He had to see Christiana, to reassure himself that she was all right. He couldn't forget that moment when she had risen up out of the bushes and taken a chance with her life for him. Every time he closed his eyes he felt that lance of fear for her, that need to keep her safe. Getting up, he yanked on the robe that hung in the bathroom for unexpected and unprepared guests. The house was silent as he slipped down the hall to her room. He paused outside her door, calling himself any number of kinds of fool for coming to her in the dead of the night. He opened the door.

Christiana stared at the panel, holding her breath, and not because she was afraid. Somehow she had known he would come. The moment Pippa had told her Josh planned to insist Rich share the estate with them until the danger was passed, she had known

117

the night would not pass without them coming together. The attack had honed their passion to a need that even now sang in her body. So she had waited, a bride for her mate, a sacrifice for the desire she had never known, a woman for her man. The choices of emotions were endless; the need was not. Had he not come to her, she would have gone to him, risking her pride for his touch.

"You took long enough," she whispered, watching him walk silently toward her.

Rich barely hesitated in his approach. "You were waiting?" He hadn't expected her to be awake. Stopping beside the bed, he looked down at her. The moon painted silver shadows along her length in the silky gown that was her only covering.

"I shouldn't admit it, but I was." She lay looking up at him, waiting for his decision. "No one has ever offered up his life for me before."

"Gratitude." His whole body stiffened against the possibility he hadn't considered.

"No. Awe. Shock maybe." She smiled faintly. "I've always been the one to do the caring. My size and my profession almost make that a requirement."

He came down on the bed, touching her face, tracing the bones that formed her features. "I care. I found out how deeply tonight when I watched you risk yourself for me. Like you, I'm not used to that kind of sacrifice."

She leaned her cheek against the warmth of his hand. "Gratitude?" Her tone was a teasing mockery of his earlier question.

He smiled as his hand stroked the length of her neck to the soft swells of flesh covered in lace.

"No." He outlined the bodice gently. "I see your tents don't extend to bedroom attire."

"They did at one time. I almost strangled myself one night. I decided I like this kind of thing better."

"So do I," he murmured huskily, replacing his fingers with his lips. "Tell me I can stay."

She laughed softly, even as she arched into his mouth. Pleasure was a wave of warm sensation washing through her, softening her body, heating her blood. Her hands curved about his shoulders. "It took you long enough to ask."

He raised his head to grin down at her. His eyes glittered with desire in the light of the moon. "Demanding woman."

"Is that good?"

He untied the belt of his robe as he watched her face. He had to see every change of emotion because before this night was done, he would teach her the secrets of passion and darkness and she would give him joyfully the gift of her body. "It can be."

"For you?"

"With you, yes." He let the robe part, watching her eyes widen, hearing the soft gasp of surprise on her lips. "I want you to be anything you wish. I want to hold out my hands and sprinkle diamonds of memories into yours. Whatever the future I want no regret, no fear, no pain to mar this joining."

"You're a poet." She slipped over a few inches, hating the momentary distance between them. She sighed when Rich stood to let the robe drop before accepting her invitation to lay with her.

Rich folded her into his arms, letting her grow accustomed to his body molded to hers. "We fit, you and I. You please me very much, woman."

"And you please me, man," she whispered, letting her fingers waltz across his back, exploring the strong, sleekly drawn lines and planes. His husky groan made her more daring.

"Keep that up and going slow this first time will be the last thing on my mind," he warned even as he shifted to allow her greater access.

"I want to know what I'm getting into."

He kissed her deeply as his fingers found the buttons that ran the front length of her gown. When he raised his head, her breasts were bared to his gaze. But it was her eyes that held his attention. "Christiana Drake, you are a woman among women. A virgin who doesn't shrink or shy away. Honest need right down to your toes. Do you have any idea how special that is?" He trailed his hands over her body, touching, caressing, teasing. For the first time in his life, he wanted to talk while he made love. He wanted their minds to mate with the joining of their bodies. He wanted her to know his thoughts, his emotions. He needed to share hers.

"I thought men were quiet at a time like this," she whispered, drowning in the delight of his foreplay. Her own hands were busy, learning by imitation what pleased and stoked the flame of urgency higher.

"I'm rewriting the rule book for us," he said while his tongue swirled around each breast, stroking each nipple until it stood erect waiting for the next warm bath. As he worked down her body, his hands leading the way, he felt her breath quicken, her sentences just fragments of speech. His own voice cracked on the words he poured over her. He stroked her thighs, urging them open, easing down between them until he was poised for the first thrust.

"Look at me," he commanded roughly. "Are you ready?"

Christiana opened her eyes, staring at the taut features looming above her. Her body was on fire for him, needing his possession to put out the inferno. Her nails dug into his hips. "Do it," she demanded, arching up, offering her body as she had offered her life, with abandon, against all logic and without regret.

Her words snapped the last of Rich's control. He surged forward, piercing the veil with one clean strike. Her cry of joy and pain echoed between them, a sign neither would ever forget. He paused, his last consideration for her innocence. Her hips tightened on his, denying him even that.

"Don't stop. Take me with you."

He settled onto her, holding her tight as they rode together to the climax both craved. Their breaths mated, harsh, demanding in the silence. Their bodies gleamed with the moisture of energy fusing in the uphill battle. His voice called her name. Hers answered in a shattered call. Then light exploded for them both. The night looked on. The moon held its post beyond their window and the silence was a seamless cover to wrap them in slumber. The words were over. The possession of body, the touching of minds so complete, sleep was all that remained to share.

Christiana shifted slightly in her sleep, feeling the arm that had stayed securely around her through the night move with her. She smiled as she opened her eyes, recalling everything and reliving again that instant of possession. She turned on her side, reaching out to lightly trace Rich's lips. His eyes opened, staring straight into hers.

"You look happy."

"I am."

"No regrets?"

"No. You?"

He smiled, pulling her close for the first kiss of the morning. "Only that I dropped into a black hole of sleep when I could have shared the hours of the night with you."

"So did I. Reaction from the attack and this, probably," she whispered as she snuggled against his length.

Rich inhaled her scent, knowing as long as he lived he'd never forget it. "Sore?"

"A little." She laughed with the admission. "Very reminiscent of my first horseback ride." She nipped at his chin before taking his lips. "It was worth it. Let's do it again."

For one moment, Rich gave in to temptation; then he lifted his head, tucking her roving hands against his chest. "No, my woman. We will not do it again. I'm not that selfish and you're not that stupid." He chuckled at her glare and the sudden gleam of challenge that stole it from her eyes. "You won't get me to change my mind. I won't be here. I'm going to my room, collect one of the swimsuits I'm sure to find there, and then I'm going down to the pool."

"You wouldn't."

He kissed her quickly before slipping out of bed. "Bet?" He pulled on his robe without looking at her. His will power was stretched thin enough as it was. Tempting himself was not only dumb; it was a good way to give in. Heading for the door, he added, "Move it, pretty diver. I have an urge to see you flying against a dawn sky."

"Poet," she accused huskily as the door shut behind him. Christiana didn't waste time as she surged out of bed, feeling better in spite of her complaining muscles than she had ever felt in her life. She was downstairs in record time, but even so, he beat her in the water.

The sky was a pewter mist over the land, the air soft with dew and the silence of the slowly fading darkness. She stopped at the edge of the pool, inhaling deeply, letting the morning cast its magic over the day. She looked down at Rich, her lips curved into a smile that invited him to share her happiness. As he tread water watching her, Rich knew then what he should have known the night before. He was perilously close to falling in love with this woman. The emotions pulling at him right now were more intense than those he had ever experienced with any of his three wives. Every instinct for self-preservation demanded he protect himself. Every need of his mind and his body commanded he give them a chance. Ever a gambler, he chose the latter without another thought.

"Race you," he called, suddenly needing to run if only for a moment.

Christiana responded to the challenge, for her own reasons needing the mind-focusing demand of a contest. She dove from where she stood, coming to the surface in a racing crawl that shot her through the water just as Rich took off beside her. Diving was

her gift, but she was no amateur at speed-swimming.
In an instant, the race, man to woman, was on.

*   *   *

"You are turning into a nosy woman, Pippa
Luck," Josh whispered, stopping behind his wife and
slipping his arms around her naked length. He drew
her against his bare chest, staring out at the pool
stretched below them. Rich and Christiana were racing each other, two long bodies cleaving through the
water with the precision of well-oiled and tuned
machines.

"They look good together," Pippa said softly, before turning in her husband's arms. "You might as
well start ordering my lavender Maserati today."

He kissed the triumphant smile from her lips.
"They aren't at the altar yet, my love. Don't try to
collect on a wager you haven't even won."

"You are a stubborn man," she crooned, her
hands slipping over the body she had come to know
so well. His groan of pleasure at her touch sent a
shaft of desire sliding into her soul. It was always
this way between them. "That's going to make my
victory all the sweeter."

"Someone has to try to hold out against you," he
returned, lifting her into his arms and carrying her
to their bed.

"Ready to give in?" Rich called, treading water.
Christiana shook the hair out of her eyes. "I
should never have tried to keep up with you," she
gasped, laughing. "That will teach me my ego is
bigger than my brain."

Rich chuckled as he stroked toward her. "Honey,
nothing about you is big." He pulled her to him,

keeping them afloat with his legs. "You're beautifully curved in all the places a man dreams about. You're tall enough so I don't end up with a crick in my neck just by kissing you. I didn't lose you in the sheets last night."

"You're terrible," she giggled, feeling younger than she had ever felt in her life. "Lost in the sheets, indeed."

He kissed the tip of her nose, then her mouth. "Stop trying to seduce me with that gurgle and get on that board. I have dreams of you on that thing, wrapped in the dawn, poised on the edge of nothing."

The humor between them slipped into its new guise. Desire. Intimacy. Warmth. She touched his face, reading the sincerity written there. No one had ever described her or the skill she loved so much with such beauty. "Thank you."

"For what? The truth?"

"For seeing it like that."

"*You*, not *it*."

"You make me feel so many things I've never felt before."

"Your mother should have warned you that kind of honesty to a man is like handing him an edge on a platter."

"I'm not afraid of what's between us. Maybe it would be better if I were. I'd run then."

"I don't want you afraid or running."

"I like that, too. You're the first man who hasn't acted intimidated around me or grabbed for what didn't belong to him."

"I have always preferred strength to mush. It takes

too much energy to grab. I'd much rather spend it in more pleasurable ways."

Tipping back her head, she laughed for the sheer joy of it. "What an expression."

Rich stared at her face, the long line of her throat. Touching his lips to the exposed length, he drew patterns of kisses from her chin to the hollow where her pulse raced for him. "Yours is much better, beautiful, full of life and fire." His tongue traced the outline of the top of her suit, the chlorine losing its taste in the richness of her skin.

Christiana wrapped her arms around him, wanting more of the warmth. "We should stop. We both have to get dressed for work," she whispered, holding his head to her. Her eyes were half closed against the pale light of the rising sun.

"We put in a lot of overtime last night. I claim the right of comp time."

"Reasonable."

"I'm always reasonable," he murmured, drawing the suit down so that the edge just covered her nipples. "I think I will buy you a bikini. Will you let me?" Lifting his head, he kissed her deeply before she could answer.

Christiana met his kiss, taking as much as he gave. Her body was heating to his touch, learning his ways, wanting more than it had known. A hungry thing, a demanding instrument that no longer allowed her to control it without question. Her hands loved the feel of his hair, the power of his muscles under her fingers. "I've never had one," she breathed, barely conscious enough of the words to answer.

"Yellow, I think."

Christiana stared at his lips, needing to taste them

again. The words distracted her. "I don't care what color it is. Kiss me."

"No." He pulled her tight against him, hoping the pressure of her flesh molded to his would cage the pain of need that was tearing into his soul. "I'm not playing any longer. I want you too damn much. Help me to remember this pool is not the place."

Christiana froze in his arms, the golden haze of desire fading slowly at the desperate fight for control in his expression. "You pick the worst times to say no," she breathed, leaning her cheek against his shoulder. "I don't want to stop." Holding on to him helped to ease the ache. "I want to forget that there is anyone in this world but us."

Rich's arms tightened around her, her confession all that he had ever wanted to hear on a woman's lips. "Hold that thought."

She raised her head. "For how long?"

"Tonight."

"Again?"

"We're adults. Do you really think Josh or Pippa will mind?"

"No." She smiled faintly. "I guess I still have a few hang-ups to get over."

"It's no easier for me. Remember, we're in this together. We share. I need that."

She touched his cheek. He had given her so much that it would have been easy to give him this for his own sake alone. "So do I."

"What do you mean they're in jail? How?" The woman's voice was thick with rage, frustration, and a kind of dangerous excitement. The man watching her pace the floor frowned but did nothing to stop the restless movements.

"I mean those fools had a perfect setup. They fixed Richland's tire so that it would blow out on command of a remote-control device. All they had to do was follow him and that woman at a safe distance, wait for a deserted area, and flip a switch. It should have been a piece of cake. Instead they let themselves be taken out by a nanny and a soft-fingered playboy."

"You don't know Rich."

He laughed harshly, his eyes traveling over the long length of the well-cared-for feminine body before him. "And you do. But bedroom knowledge is no help here."

"What do we do now?"

"Hire some real pros. We'll need them. Thanks to those fools Dingo and Rollo, Luck and his cohorts are on their guard. Besides, I want that nanny. No one, least of all a woman, makes a fool of me."

Rich shut the door to Josh's study and followed the older man across the room to the large desk, its back to the river-view windows. Every instinct warned that time was running out. "The in-depth security checks should be done today."

"But you don't expect them to turn up anything."

"No. Whoever is doing this knows his stuff. I think the culprit is buried too deep for something this simple to yank him out of the shadows. What I want to do is a little stalking of my own. I'm tired of waiting. I've notified the pilot to ready the Lear for a trip to Tennessee. I'll finish up in Arizona."

Josh inclined his head, his expression somber.

"Agreed. Just keep in constant contact and don't stay out any longer than absolutely necessary. And watch your back."

Rich's smile was dangerous and totally controlled. "I intend to live to be an old man."

Josh gave a short crack of unamused laughter. "I have a friend I'd like to call in while you're out of town. He has some contacts who might be able to do some underground looking for us."

Undisturbed by the suggestion, Rich nodded. "I'm prepared to accept any help we can get. I don't want any variation or repeat of what happened in the woods. I don't want the women or the twins in this a second longer than necessary. The sooner our nemesis is out of commission the happier we'll all be."

"Any more ideas about what tender spot you might have touched without knowing it."

"No," Rich said flatly, making no effort to mask his disgust and frustration. "Between that and Christiana, I didn't get much sleep last night. To say the least, my timing is the pits."

Josh laughed. "I don't think timing between men and women was ever intended to be on the same schedule. I remember having the same reaction when I ran into Pippa."

Rich gave a reluctant chuckle then sobered. "This project is too important for me to be distracted."

Josh didn't try to be kind. "You aren't the type to give less than total commitment. I'm not worried. Besides, you aren't the only one involved."

"Damned with faint praise."

"I try." He picked up a single sheet of paper and slid it across the desk. The message had arrived from his brother in the early hours of the morning. The information it contained had held a shock that he was just now coming to accept. He had no idea how Rich would take the news.

Rich glanced at it curiously. "What's this?"

"Read it."

Obeying, Rich scanned the handwritten words. "He can't be serious."

"Joe doesn't play around with stuff like this. His sight is rarely off and he is positive Kay has a lot to do with this situation. He sent the note by messenger while you and Christiana were in the pool."

"Do you believe it?"

Josh had no intention of hitting Rich in what he knew was still a tender spot, so he chose his words with care. "I've learned not to disbelieve. And we really don't have any other clues at the moment. I don't think we can afford to overlook his input."

Rich stared at the sheet that listed his third ex-wife as the source of the threat in which they were all involved. "Kay? I'll grant you my ex is no one's idea of Mary Poppins, but a thief and a party to attempted murder? What's more, she doesn't even have any family, much less someone with underworld connections."

"As far as you know. I don't imagine she goes around announcing it. I sent one of our security people to check her apartment out. He hasn't had time to get back to me yet." He sighed roughly. "Joe's sight might not stand up in court and we both know it. But it could give us an edge."

Josh was right. Kay could have any number of family and had just chosen not to mention their existence. One of the main problems in their marriage had been her incredible ability to lie at will over anything. Added to that, Kay possessed inside work-ing knowledge of Luck Enterprises and worst of all, she carried a grudge over the fact that Rich had been the one to seek a divorce on the grounds of infidelity, her gambling, and her complete indifference to start-ing the family that he had wanted so much. He raised his head to find Josh watching him with no expres-sion discernible on his face. He knew how sensitive Josh was to any slights against Joe. He knew how much Luck Enterprises meant to him. And he knew what it had cost Josh to be honest with him about Kay's possible involvement and the source from which the information had come.

"Thank Joe for me. I hope he's wrong, but I'll go on the assumption he's right."

Josh released his breath in a deep sigh. "Thanks."

Rich rose. "I'll call you as soon as I reach the Tennessee plant," he said before he left. Closing the door behind him, he went upstairs to find Christiana. For one second the image of the sleek golden-haired Kay the last time he had seen her imposed itself over Christiana's more earthy appeal. The two could not have been more opposite. Christiana was everything the older woman wasn't. Christiana was real, honest, and strong. She gave rather than took. She offered a man warmth in the center of the night and laughter in the silver light of the dawn. She was the calm to smooth the stress from the day and the fire to burn the need from his body. He smiled for one moment, forgetting the danger that stalked them as he paused outside the nursery door, hearing her laugh mingle with that of the twins. Kay had been dross, but Christiana was pure gold. Rich knocked on the door of the nursery, his eyes molten with tenderness and a depth of emotion that was growing with every moment in her company.

"Come in," Christiana called, glancing up from the educational video the twins were playing. Expecting Pippa, her brows rose when she saw Rich. The look in his eyes sent a soft wave of color sweeping over her fair skin. "I thought you would have left the house by now," she murmured, dragging her gaze from his just long enough to check that the children were engrossed in their game.

"I should have been," he said quietly, moving to her side but not touching her.

She got to her feet, reaching past the tenderness and the memories of his look to the worry beneath. "What's wrong?" she asked, drawing him to the alcove and the chairs near the window.

The small seclusion allowed him the luxury of touching her, his fingers lightly tracing her jaw to her lips. The need to kiss her was so powerful that it was almost more than his control could take. "I'm going to be leaving town for a few days. I don't want to, and if it were anything else but this, I would give the job to someone else."

Disappointment was a sharp thorn. Christiana absorbed the pain without letting any of it show on her face. He had work to do and she would not take his thoughts from that job. The danger to himself and others was too great. She wrapped her hand around his wrist, feeling his pulse beat beneath the tips of her fingers. "I wish you didn't have to go, but I understand that you must."

"There will be time for us," he murmured, stunned at the caring he saw reflected in her eyes.

No one had ever given him such acceptance without demand.

She smiled faintly. "I know. That wasn't what I meant. I don't like you being out there on your own."

Rich stilled, staring into her clear eyes, hearing her words all the way to his starving soul. She meant it. He could see her disappointment, and yet stronger than that was her anxiety for his safety. He leaned forward, needing to kiss her as he had needed few things in his life. "You're a miracle, my swan. A gorgeous miracle for a man who doesn't believe in them." His lips settled softly on hers, reverence in his touch that had never been.

Christiana sighed gently as she swayed closer. His hands on her shoulders held her near but not flesh-to-flesh. She opened her eyes, looking straight into his. "I'll miss you," she breathed.

"You'd better. Because I sure will be missing you, woman." He took her mouth one final time, this kiss holding all the wanting he would save for her for the moment when they could be together. "Remember where we left off," he added before releasing her and striding through the door without a backward look.

NINE

"As you can see, Mr. Richland, there is absolutely no way anyone could get in or out of the plant without alerting one of the guards. The dogs and their handlers are even changed on a random basis so that no one could get to one of the men with a bribe."

"No security system is foolproof," Rich inserted dryly, privately agreeing with the manager of the plant.

William Carey allowed himself a faint smile. One did not antagonize one's superiors, especially when that superior was clearly jumping at shadows. "I hardly think our facility is the first line of attack anyway. The formula is the only thing that makes our burner usable. Without it . . ." He spread his hands, letting the silence finish his sentence.

Rich glanced through the man, knowing his thoughts and not caring at this point. Carey was right about one thing. Security here was tight, tougher than he remembered. Only someone who was familiar with the operation of Luck Enterprises could have gotten to the plans for the burner. The memory of the moment when he had first wondered if the plans hadn't been duplicated still stung. The strange way the complete set had been missing for about two hours three weeks ago had passed everyone's notice until his descent on the plant. Even now, questioning of all available personnel was being set up.

"Has Kay been around lately?" Rich asked suddenly.

The man stared at him in surprise. "I haven't seen her if she has," Carey replied, looking confused. "Is she working for the company again?"

Rich shook his head. "I want to know if she makes any attempt to enter the facility. Or if she sends anyone here for any reason. Make certain all the men at the gates know. No slips." He glanced back at the lists of visitors he had been scanning without success. The precautions were twofold in purpose. One, he couldn't be positive the plans had been compromised and two, he didn't want the culprits to tumble to the fact he had noted the missing hours if they had been copied. "Also, I want two men at every station from this moment on. Double teams in the building at all times and a thorough search of anyone, including his mode of transport from tire to roof, entering or leaving the compound. And that includes trunks, underchassis, the works."

Carey gaped at him. "Do you know how many people work at this plant? The traffic in the mornings and at the end of the day will be impossible. I'll be lucky if I don't have the job stewards down on my back."

Rich focused on the man. Hard purpose and fierce determination to ward off this threat turned the tawny depths to lethal yellow gold. "You earn the six-figure salary to do more than sit behind that desk in your office. This is a crisis situation for Luck Enterprises. Don't end up being the man who blew our plans out of the water. I don't think Joshua Luck will take it as a favor, and I have a long memory."

Gulping, Carey took a step back. In his short stint with Luck Enterprises, he had been exposed only to Martin Richland's urbane, smooth side. He had never faced this sharp-eyed commander. "It will be taken care of immediately," he agreed quickly, hoping his capitulation would be enough to let him off the hook.

Rich inclined his head, expecting nothing else. Carey had come highly recommended and had certainly improved the productivity of the plant as well as supervising the prototype burner. Under normal conditions Rich would have used tact rather than power to get the job done. But time had run out, and with it the luxury of softer methods.

Christiana sat on the floor, playing with the twins although her mind was on Rich. The time to analyze her feelings was fast approaching. She had entered into a relationship with Rich, knowing the risks and accepting the benefits. But this morning she had learned something she had been too blind to see before. She was falling in love with a man who had every reason not to believe or trust the emotion. When it had only been desire driving them together, she had thought she could handle their affair. Passion, no matter how beautiful, eventually burned itself out. But not love, at least not for her. She would carry the memories and the scars of parting, as part they must with Rich feeling the way he did about commitment, to her grave. The knowledge was frightening. A light knock on the door drew her attention, momentarily scattering her fears.

She turned, calling, "Come in."

Pippa poked her head around the door. "Tell me you'd like company."

Christiana's brows rose at the odd, almost pleading note in the older woman's voice. "Definitely." She waved a hand at the engrossed children. "Pick your spot."

Pippa plopped down on the floor as her son grinned at her. "I couldn't write." She shrugged in frustration. "It's crazy, but I'm worried. I don't like this situation. And I hate sitting on the sidelines not knowing what's going on."

"So do I." Christiana hesitated, then added, "It's not as though either of them need us to worry." She tried a faint smile that attempted to look relaxed but failed. The edges trembled with the anxiety she would rather have hidden. "I think I'm giving myself away. And even that doesn't seem to matter. We could have been killed last night."

Pippa traded her look for look. "That is still true. Do you want out?"

Christiana looked at the children whom she was coming to love. Her training and talents could mean the difference between harm and safety. Running away would leave them unprotected. Then there was Rich. She had come too far to walk away until she had to. "No. Until the danger is over I won't leave the twins," she said definitely.

Pippa stared at her, trying to see past Christiana's unruffled expression. Her instincts said that Christiana was hurting in some subtle way that had nothing to do with the attempt on her and Rich's life. "Is that the only reason?" she probed delicately.

Christiana hesitated. Suddenly she knew she desperately needed to talk, to find an answer, if there were one, for her and Rich. "No," she said carefully.

"If you want an ear, I'll be glad to listen." Pippa shrugged, her lips curving slightly. "I'm fairly good with problems, especially people ones."

"It isn't a problem exactly."

Pippa scanned Christiana's face, seeing the knowledge that she had hoped to find. "You love him."

"How did you . . ?" Her voice trailed off as she laughed uncomfortably. "I hope he doesn't see that in me. I have a feeling he'd run a mile."

"Probably. Kay cut him up into little pieces and threw him to the vultures. I don't think he believes in love anymore, or if he does, he sees it as less than it can be."

"Which leaves me in a terrible situation. I thought I could handle an affair. I could have, too, if all I felt was passion. But love means marriage and children to me, two things I would give my life to possess. I want Rich as my husband and a father to our children. And that stuns me because it seems like only yesterday that we met."

"I knew I intended to have Josh in my life permanently somewhere around the second hour. He just took a lot of convincing."

"I never thought I was the kind of woman to be swept off her feet. It seems that I was wrong."

"The unromantic type. Too mature for the high of instant attraction. I remember feeling like that."

Christiana's brows rose. "I don't believe it."

"I had more reason than you. I'd been touched by passion and found it mild, interesting, but not something I had to hold on to. My life was full of other people, some fictional, others real. I didn't need. I think that's the thing that makes anyone change a certain way of life. As long as something satisfies a need, why look for something new. And age. The great badge of time passage. I'm too old for whatever. Whoever first said that should have been strangled at birth." She reached out to stroke the cowlick on the back of her son's head. "Should I have denied myself this for some stupid age myth? Should I have walked away from Josh and the life we have created together because I was in my forties, too old to feel that fire-hot lick of real, honest desire, that need to mate for always? Emotion doesn't know or care how old your body is. It only hears your heart, and once in a while, your mind. Believe that and you can do anything. Even convince a man who has no reason to trust women or their emotions that you love him above all others and you will give yourself only to him for all time."

Christiana stared at and through Pippa, thinking over her words, knowing deep in her soul that her answer lay in the older woman's wisdom. "I have always loved a challenge," she murmured to herself.

Pippa smiled wickedly. "I told Josh you'd pull it off," she said, laughing.

Christiana focused on Pippa's face. "What are you up to?" she demanded, having gotten a measure of Pippa's convoluted mind days before.

"You'll have to promise not to be shocked if I tell you."

"I promise."

"I win a lavender Masarati, which my darling, overly cautious husband is positive will land him in court in record time if you can get Rich to the altar."

Christiana stared at her, torn between laughing aloud at Pippa's daring and strangling her for her maneuvering. "You have a bet on us?" Christiana demanded, wanting to be certain she hadn't misunderstood.

Pippa nodded. "Stop looking so scandalized. I haven't played any tricks, and Rich is well aware of my reputation as a matchmaker for the most unlikely candidates. I'm surprised he hasn't told you."

"He did."

"You should have believed him. I like seeing people mated with their other halves. Life is too empty when spent alone. I care about Rich, and the moment I met you I felt I would want you for a friend. You have everything that he needs and he understands you better than any other male ever can. I have been there. Have I done so badly by arranging a meeting? Is your life not richer for having allowed Rich to touch your heart? Is his life not warmer for having reached out to you?" She faced Christiana, not afraid of her judgment. "I play games. Life can be boring without them. But I never hurt anyone without just cause."

Put that way, Christiana couldn't deny Pippa's truth. Whatever traces of anger had risen in her drifted away. Her lips twitched as she stared into the too-serious pale eyes. "Knowing how Rich feels about marriage, either you're an incurable optimist or blind," Christiana murmured, shaking her head. "What's more, I don't know anyone else who would have the nerve to make this kind of bet and then admit it.''

Pippa shrugged gracefully. "Life is over too soon for running for cover, playing without enjoying it and for being cautious. Why be ordinary when extraordinary is so damn much fun?" She popped to her feet and swung her son into her arms then around in a circle. "The only way I'll ever die is if Death is a lot faster than I am." Pippa stopped, laughing, with the child in her arms. She turned her head, her eyes belying the smile on her face. "You're aren't angry?"

"I should be."

"But you aren't."

"Being around you is probably contagious."

"That sounds like something Josh or Rich would have said. See how great my instincts are. I knew you would fit right in the first time I saw you."

"Just so long as you remember that if Rich and I don't come through, you don't get your Masarati."

"I have faith."

"Like I said, an optimist or blind." Christiana rose, picking up Lori. "Well, Mama, do you want to help me get this pair down for a nap or are you going to try writing again?"

Pippa grimaced. "Is that a shot in the dark or am I that transparent?"

"You're definitely not transparent."

"I needed something to take my mind off Josh being out there. I keep remembering how easily a bullet can find its target. Unless our nemesis knows the ins and outs of Josh's business he might think killing or seriously injuring Josh would hamper the project long enough for it to be stolen."

"I agree."

"I would have rather you hadn't. These visions that Joe keeps having aren't helping."

"What visions?"

"Rich didn't tell you?" Pippa frowned. "I wonder why."

"I can think of several reasons and none of them is palatable."

"I sense a feminine uprising in the making."

"Call it talking some sense into one overprotective male." Christiana moved to the bathroom to wash Lori's hands and face. Pippa repeated the procedure with J. Jr. "You should have seen him after I whacked Dingo in the back with that wrench. You would have thought he would be pleased that one of them was out of commission, but all he seemed to be was angry."

"Relief makes funny emotions."

"So he said. But I think he secretly wants this frail type of woman that I couldn't be on my best day."

"I think you're reading him wrong, but if you aren't, teach him better. The first time Josh saw me, he thought I was trying to pick him up."

"You're joking."

"No." Pippa grinned wickedly. "Actually I was, but I'm not about to admit it now. I hate people, especially males, who say I told you so."

"Tell me." When Pippa hesitated, Christiana added persuasively, "It will keep both our minds occupied. I'm no more excited about letting Rich know how badly this is getting to me than you are."

"Best argument you could have used. Let's get these little terrors into bed, then we'll retire to the pool and I'll give you the line and verse of our so-called courtship.''

Rich entered his hotel room, feeling discouraged, an unusual emotion for him. He had found absolutely nothing out of the ordinary, nothing to substantiate his belief that the plans had been compromised. The security chief for Luck Enterprises who had accompanied him on this fact-finding mission had the same report. It was like working in the dark with no available light source. There was only so much they could do without clues. Even Kay had apparently sunk out of sight without a trace. He shrugged out of his jacket, glancing at the clock. He had time for a quick shower before he called Christiana. Just thinking of her made the day a little less frustrating in some ways and more so in others. Right now he would have been home, talking to her, holding her in his arms. Without knowing it, his expression lightened slightly as he walked naked into the bath. They would have had dinner, talking with Josh and Pippa, and then gone upstairs to the silence and privacy of one of their rooms. He would touch her, feel her body soften, catch fire just for him. The ache he felt now would grow, but relief would be only a kiss, a touch, a word away.

''Damn,'' he swore savagely as he fought the images that for now could only exist in his mind. But for this damn mess with the formula, he and Christiana could be together. Damn Kay, he thought as he twisted off the faucets and stepped out of the stall to yank a towel around his body. He didn't care what time it was. He was calling her now. Stalking to the phone, he punched in a series of numbers. Seconds later he heard her voice.

"It's not seven," Christiana said, making no effort to disguise her delight in hearing from him.

"I couldn't wait." He hadn't meant to tell her that, but he didn't regret his honesty. "It has been a rotten day. Tell me something good about it."

Christiana sighed, thinking about how much she missed him and how little she understood exactly what, if anything besides desire, he was feeling for her. "I wish I could." The sudden flatness of her tone warned her to be careful. Deliberately lightening her words, she added, "Unless you'd like to hear that Lori has managed to stand on her head."

Entangled in his own emotional web, Rich missed the subtleties. He sat on the bed, dabbing at his chest with the end of the towel. He smiled faintly, relaxing as he hadn't all day. "I suppose J. Jr. is learning to hang from the chandelier?"

"Not yet. But I live in hope. The little rascal." Christiana settled into the chair beside the bed, loving the sound of his husky drawl. Moments before she had felt so lonely, so alone. Now the silence was filled with the man.

"Did I catch you in the middle of something?"

"No, I was just changing to have a swim before dinner."

Rich noted the tense. Without warning, with the glory of their passion as a memory, his mind supplied visions of a nude Christiana in the pool. No ordinary swimsuit hid her fabulous body from his view. Only the water, she, and he existed in his fantasy. He slipped into the pool with her, stroking to her side, smiling as she smiled at his approach.

He reached out his hand, his eyes on the mauve tips of her breasts. He inhaled deeply, feeling his body respond to the erotic daydream. Sanity returned in a heartbeat. He shook his head to dispel the tantalizing image, but it hung on, perhaps knowing how much he needed the illusion to be reality.

"Rich, are you still there?" Christiana asked as the silence lengthened.

"I'm here," he managed through gritted teeth. A full-grown man, with reasonable control, did not have this kind of reaction to thinking of a naked woman, he reminded himself as he fought his body for supremacy.

"Is something wrong? You sound strange."

I sound aroused, he thought with grim humor, having no intention of telling her that. Honesty could only go so far. He had never had a woman tie him up in knots before. Daily, Christiana was teaching him things about her sex that he didn't know, understand, or have any defense against. Confusion spawned evasion. Need created wariness, and emotion demanded camouflage. "It's been a rotten day with one thing and another," he said instead. Her disappointed sigh cut through his barriers, pulling the truth out of him. "I wish I were there with you." Once the words were spoken, he wondered if she would use them against him as the women in his past had.

Christiana shivered at the husky sincerity in his words. "I wish you were, too."

He waited for more. When nothing came, he added slowly, feeling his way, "I needed that."

"You made it easy."

He hadn't known he could react so strongly to her

admiration, drinking her words as a man dying in the desert would gulp water. "I thought I would hate being vulnerable again."

Christiana touched the phone with her free hand, stroking the mouthpiece, wishing it were his lips. His admission pulled one from her. "I'm scared."

He didn't pretend to misunderstand. "So am I."

"I thought watching you drive away this morning, knowing that someone wanted a formula enough to kill you for it, was difficult, but this is more so."

"Promise you'll stay inside the compound."

"Will you promise to hide as well?"

"You know I can't. I have to find that guy."

"And I have to do my job. If it takes me away from the protection of these walls, you have to trust me to do my best to take care of myself and the children if necessary."

Suddenly the conversation took a different turn, a turn into areas that both had skirted. The silence stretched out, fraught with a need of reassurance.

Rich looked into the future, perhaps the blackness that Joe had foretold. Suddenly he saw Christiana in danger far greater than their attack. In his arrogance and passion he had missed the most vital clue of all. A woman who had waited this long for someone special in her life didn't succumb to a sudden fire-hot desire unless the emotions driving her were more complex than simple gratification of a physical need. Love. As sure as he was breathing, he knew Christiana loved him. As the knowledge twisted in his gut, he learned his own truth. He loved her.

Desire had made him gently breach her defenses. Caring had made him worry about the danger in which she stood because of him. But neither could have driven a stake of regret, futility, and pain in his heart. Christiana had come to him in innocence. He had brought her nothing but his shopworn touch and a bag of memories that made complete trust in her or their future together impossible. He had learned of heaven in her arms, held his dreams in his hands for one shining moment. But now he felt the sands of those illusions slipping through his fingers, the dawn sliding into a darkness more complete than any he had known. The past had taught him hard lessons. But Christiana had given him the most painful and the most glorious of all. She was not a woman for half measures—half a man, half a heart. He couldn't forget what he had become. He couldn't match her innocence of heart. He sighed deeply, tensing against the severing of the tie between them that he would have to make. Words were swords, the only ones he had.

"You're right, of course. I, better than most, should know how capable you are of taking care of yourself. You took on our attackers without batting an eye. I don't know why I worried," Rich said finally, slowly, knowing that Christiana would color his response with her own interpretation.

Christiana inhaled sharply at the bite of his words. She had thought he understood her, had been proud of her, had accepted her for what she was. Fear touched her stealthily, slipping through the beauty of the passion he had shown her to the uncertainties and doubts beneath.

Rich waited for her to snap back. When she didn't, he cursed silently. "I've got to go. I've got a lot of work to do tonight. I can't afford to be distracted right now."

The fear coalesced into one terrible pain. "This sounds remarkably like a good-bye," she said, refusing to allow his vague references to stand unchallenged.

His features twisted in agony, Rich readied himself for the final blow. "It is. What we had was special." Even to protect her from himself he couldn't destroy the moments they had shared. "But it isn't enough for me. And it shouldn't be for you."

The word seared her tongue. "Why?"

"I'm no good at a permanent commitment like marriage."

"I haven't asked you to marry me," she pointed out, digging deep into her reserves, praying he wouldn't realize that she was slowly bleeding to death inside.

Angered at his own blind acceptance that Christiana could even enter the class of long-term but uncommitted relationships that had been his mode of operation since his last divorce, Rich snapped, "And you won't, either. You deserve better than a three-time loser with three women cluttering up his life. I never should have let myself think about you. All I've done is pull you into danger of one kind or another. I took what you have been saving for someone who would really matter to you. I gave you nothing that I haven't given others and had it tossed back in my face."

Christiana closed her eyes against the finality in his voice and the harsh summation of a time so perfect, so filled with emotion that she still hadn't the words to describe all that he had given her. "I have asked you for nothing."

"Then we're both fools. You should have, woman.

You should have.'' Without another word he hung up.

Christiana replaced the receiver, not even realizing that for the first time in her life, she was crying. Tears, endless, silent trickles of grief flowed over her skin, heating the cold flesh for the woman hurting too much to scream in pain. Wrapping her arms around her waist, she held on to the only tangible in her life. Herself. She had survived so much to reach this point. The one thing she had coveted and never thought to have for one brief moment had been within her reach. Her own special someone to live with, to love with, to grow old with. Her face twisted in lines of agony and defeat. But Fate, that macabre mistress, had always denied her its bounty. Once again she faced an empty future, destined to be filled only with the children of others, images of happiness such as Pippa and Josh shared, the only touch of the heaven men and women gave to each other. For her, Rich was her mate. If not he, then no other.

TEN

"Richland is in Arizona. So far it looks as though our contacts inside are safe. We've got a copy of the burner plans, but we still don't have the formula." Nick stared out the window of the penthouse, glaring at the skyline that had pushed the residence into the upper levels of the real-estate market.

Kay moved to the bar. In spite of the late-morning hour, she felt the need of a drink. When her cousin turned those pale eyes on her, she knew fear as an acid taste on her tongue.

"You'll have to see Richland. Get close to him." Nick turned, eyeing her elegant length with cold precision.

She shivered, watching him as one would a cobra with a flared head. Even as a child she had feared him. "How?"

"Find a way."

"You know what he thinks of me. He won't let me get close to him. Besides, that nanny seems to have his eye at the moment. Rich always was a one-woman-at-a-time man.''

"You're the one griping about the attempted murder," he reminded her brutally, laughing softly when she paled. "It's either you or a shot in the dark."

"I can't. Even if I get close to him, I won't get near that formula. Rich is too smart for that. Why won't you listen to me?"

He rose and walked to her side. "I do listen. We wouldn't be this close to making millions if I had not. But you aren't delivering. You said we would be able to get to the formula using the knowledge you had of Luck Enterprises."

"I got you the burner," she said unevenly, trying not to jerk away and showing him her fear.

"Correction. You got me into the plant and I got the burner. Without the formula it's worth about ten percent of the rest." His voice held her as much a prisoner as her own greed.

She pulled away, desperately seeking another alternative. "Maybe Rich isn't the best place to hit. There is still Joshua Luck."

"Bodyguards and that river estate with an eight-foot fence, guard dogs, and security at the gate. What's the matter, afraid you haven't got enough of what it takes to entice Richland away from his big-boned nanny," he taunted.

She whirled around, glaring at him. Suddenly she knew just how to give Nick what he wanted, to hurt Rich for dumping her, get the money, and protect herself.

"You want a way to get the formula. I'll give you one. Kidnap the children."

He stared at her, his mind ticking over the possibilities. "How?"

"Put a watch on the house. That nanny has to take them out sometime. She likes the water. The property goes all the way down to the river. There isn't any fence on that side. A fast boat with a couple of your pros could easily snatch the brats right out of that woman's arms. We ransom them for the formula."

"Luck isn't the kind of man to cave in at a threat," he observed almost gently.

"He's a blind fool over that woman he married. Those kids are his heirs. I'll bet you he would lie down in front of a truck for them."

"Theatrical, but possibly correct from all I've heard. What about Richland?"

"He's Josh's friend. He won't do anything Josh doesn't want him to do. Plus my ex has a real soft spot for kids."

He took a turn around the room, thinking over the plan. "All right. It could work. It had better work. It's going to be expensive and take time to set up."

"Better make it fast. You said yourself the buyers were getting antsy." She smiled nastily as she returned the taunt he had tossed at her about her sexuality. Each of them had their weakness.

He glared. She laughed, the fear sliding into the darkness of her convenient memory.

Rich entered Josh's office late in the afternoon, two days after. He hadn't bothered going out to the house or even by his apartment from the airport. He was tired from restless nights, plagued by images of Christiana and the future that should be possible and wasn't, and discouraged with the problem that had

sent him out of town. One small lead was no head-
way at all to his thinking. He said as much to Josh
as he dropped into a chair with a rough sigh.

"We caught the guard who let someone into the
Tennessee plant. Apparently he had been seeing a
woman who matches Kay's description and when
she asked him to allow her cousin to stop in at the
plant to pick up something he had left behind when
he was laid off, the man was too besotted to question
the idea. Nick sauntered in and out with a copy of
the plans. End of story. The guard didn't know any
more than that. We went back through the employment records and found that Nick had been in on the
burner concept almost from the beginning. And he
got his job on a bogus recommendation from me."

Josh ignored the last part of the information to
concentrate on the more important first section. "So
they've got half of what they need."

"If it hadn't been for Joe's sight we might still be
hunting in the dark."

"I'll tell Joe you said that." Josh shook his head.
"Damn! Since they have the burner, the formula is
definitely in jeopardy. The question is how will they
strike."

"There's no way to tell. All we can do is keep a
tight lid on everything, watch our backs and keep
looking. They're the ones with a time-frame problem. Every day that goes by, the odds of us getting
our patent through improve. Once that's ours, we're
home free." He rose, stretching wearily.

Josh watched him, realizing the exhaustion in
Rich's face had its roots in more than the fuel project
situation. "You look almost as washed out as she
does."

Rich stiffened, eyeing Josh warily. "Stay out of it, Josh."

"Can't. It's my house and it's bothering Pippa."

"It's *our* problem." He started for the door. Making a decision to walk away from Christiana before either of them really got hurt was the hardest thing he had ever done. He wasn't ready to have his motives examined even by the best of friends.

Josh hadn't gotten where he was by being easily put off. "When are you going to stop running from your memories and your mistakes? We all make them. No one could be around Christiana without realizing she's nothing like Kay or any of her predecessors. This woman really cares. Look at her eyes. Watch her with the twins. She's known pain, rejection, and loneliness. And for whatever reason, you matter to her."

Rich turned, his eyes bright with anger and caged pain. "Don't you think I know that? It's tearing my guts out to walk away from her. I want her. Hell, who am I kidding. I love her. But I won't mess up her life with ruining mine. It wasn't so bad when both of us were aiming for an affair. But just thinking about her in that kind of relationship breaks me out in a sweat. She deserves better—a man who isn't dragging along a raft of emotional garbage to tear up her life."

"Cop out." Kindness rarely got the tough jobs of life done. Josh didn't try to soften the truth as he met Rich's eyes. "I know your self-deception as well as I knew my own. I almost lost Pippa because I was afraid to put out my hand and accept what was mine to love."

"I won't take what I can't give."

"You don't know what you're capable of giving. You've never had a real chance to see," Josh exploded irritably, losing his temper.

Rich turned his back on the words and strode out of the office, slamming the door behind him. But no amount of mind-bending control threw Josh's comments out of his thoughts. They stayed with him through the day, destroying his concentration when he needed it most. And when he rode back to the compound in the company limo two hours after Josh, he was still in a temper.

Christiana came down the stairs just as Rich opened the front door and walked in. She stopped, staring at him, trying to stop the hurt of meeting him, of knowing he was in the same house. When he had hung up on her three days before, she had hoped against hope that he would change his mind and call her again. She had picked up the phone, times without number, intending on contacting him, but she had balked at the last second. It had taken her a night of deep thought to understand the way he had walked away. His rejection took on a new light in those hours of darkness. He had given to her once again. Sacrificing his own needs for what he considered best for her. That he was wrong she couldn't tell him. That she was prepared to take whatever he could give she couldn't prove to him. That she would be there for always she couldn't guarantee. And there lay one problem. He didn't trust her. The cruelest blow of all. He didn't trust her or her emotions. He didn't believe in the future that they could share.

So she waited. Knowing she couldn't force his

wanting, and wouldn't have taken it if she could. Now he was here, looking at her as though she were a stranger, maybe even an enemy. She came down the rest of the stairs, refusing to look away from him, silently demanding that he acknowledge her. No matter what had occurred between them, it was not in her to run.

"Rich." The days since she had last seen him hadn't been kind to him. Lines were etched deeply about his mouth, his shoulders were rigid, his expression grim. "You look tired."

Rich searched her face, finally seeing the return of that serenity that he had come to associate with her. Since he had touched her life, it had been conspicuously absent. His anger slipped a notch. He was hurting and yet she seemed unaffected. He felt cheated somehow and that added tinder to his emotional fire.

"I've been on a plane or hunting for a needle in a field of hay. I'm frustrated, exhausted, and angry. And I'm not in the mood for a soft hand on my brow. I don't like failing." He stepped back a pace when she moved forward. He watched her frown, almost missing the flicker of hurt at his need for distance.

"I doubt you failed."

The quiet certainty in her words dug deep into his pain, grabbing hold of his dreams. His fingers itched to touch her, to bask in her faith, to rest against her softness just for a moment. He had never felt so alone, so needing of the strength of a woman in his life. Jamming his hands in his pockets, he fought to remember the mess he had made of his life and all the reasons why she deserved better than he. "We haven't caught the perps yet."

She smiled at the shortened police slang. "You will."

He glared.

Her lips twitched. She was getting to him. The pain of rejection eased. It was costing him to hold to his decision to force her out of his life.

"Damn it, stop looking at me like that."

Her brows rose and her smile grew into a soft laugh. "How?"

"Like some oracle who knows the secrets of the universe." Temptation was too close and he was losing his hold on his self-imposed exile.

"Now you know how I felt when we first met." She reached out, touching his chest, feeling the strong beat of his heart beneath her palm. "You had all the answers to questions I didn't know existed."

The command to step back hovered in his mind, but he couldn't move away from her hand. "Don't do this," he breathed roughly, drawing in great draughts of air through flared nostrils as though he had run a too-long race. Her scent filled him.

"Do what?" She stepped nearer.

"You know."

"But I want you. You've taught me how to want you. And how to say it out loud." Excitement rose, gilding her need with sensations brighter than gold. Her eyes meshed with his. She could read the internal fight being waged. She could feel the power he brought to bear to hold her away. The future beckoned, a bright handful of moments that would change her life forever. "Afraid to touch me? Is your memory as good as mine? Do you lie awake at night thinking of what we shared?"

"If I do touch, I won't let go. Whatever choice

you have right now will be gone." The statements were clear, slices of sound to offer either freedom to soar or death of an illusion of love. "I have never wanted a woman, loved a woman, as I love you. If I destroy your love, it won't destroy mine. I'll still fight to the end to hold you. Even if you come to hate me, I won't let you go. But I won't give you marriage. I won't watch what we have wither, sucked dry by the demands of living together." Every muscle was stiff, every nerve drawn to the point of pain. He watched her absorb the knowledge, waiting, hoping she would walk away because he no longer could and praying that she would stay because he needed her so.

Christiana stilled, her understanding of his personal demons deepening. Total commitment. Demanding, renewing, forever there. Rich was strong enough to give her either the freedom to walk alone or the chains to bind her to his side. She weighed the choices, stunned by the strength of his love and the harshness of the lessons he had learned. But she was more awed by the demand of her own love and the realities of her yesterdays. The past was just that. The past. The future and the present were all she had. All he had. He had to see that. Unless he could accept the future as an unmarked canvas of time, there would be no tomorrow for either of them.

"You're asking of me what you won't give yourself."

"Meaning?"

"I'm ignoring every instinct that tells me I can't trust our feelings for each other, that it has happened too fast, that the need is too white-hot to survive. I'm willing to take a blind leap through time and

space with you at my side. But you aren't. I don't
need marriage, but the fact that you won't think of
it for us matters. I'm not those other women. I won't
take and then leave you. And I won't paint you with
a brush of guilt for not being able to keep loving
me." She hadn't planned her words, but as soon as
she said them and saw their effect on Rich, she knew
that she had hit on the truth. Tears of grief for the
death of her hope filled her eyes. Rich had taught
her how to cry.

His hands came out of his pockets then, stunned
by the tears and the pain she made no effort to hide.
He drew her close, expecting resistance and getting
none. "Don't," he groaned.

Her forehead resting against his heart, Christiana
tried to stem the flow of moisture. Out of grief came
anger. She would not give up. "Damn you. Think.
Trust us. Yourself. Me. Fight for us. Help me fight
for us. I won't let you do this. I can't let you do
this. It's my life, too, and I want it all."

"You can't stop me."

She raised her head. "I can." She pushed away
from his warmth, suddenly knowing what she would
do. It was a mad gamble when she had never trusted
Fate. "All right. You want an idealized mistress, I
accept. We can start now, this minute. We have time
before dinner. Come upstairs with me. Forget your
stupid scruples about what you think I deserve and
take me as I will take you. I dare you to give yourself
to me."

With every sentence, Rich's face grew sterner,
more angry. She didn't mean it. "You're crazy."

Christiana faced his temper with her own. Recklessness was almost as heady as desire, she discov-

ered. "Afraid?" She touched him, her fingers sliding over his chest, digging into the fabric of his shirt.

Rich caught her wrists, his muscles flexing in pleasure that he couldn't suppress. "For a virgin you sure learned how to be blunt about certain things in a hurry."

She wouldn't back down. "I had a good teacher."

"Well, school is out."

He was stronger than even she had thought. There was only one more chance left. "You want me to get another teacher?"

The taunt caught him on the raw. Before he could stop himself, he yanked her into his arms, glaring down at her, reading the purpose in her blazing eyes. She would do it, he realized in shock. "You do and I'll find you before you can do one damn thing to this body, pull you home by your hair and tan your bottom. Taking a lover because you want one is one thing. Taking one to get even with me you won't do," he growled, fighting every sense that said take her and make every moment count.

Christiana stroked his jaw, her voice soft but no less laced with steel. "Then you'd better take me. Because I've just decided I'm tired of having you run from me."

"You wouldn't."

"Try me."

"You'd only hurt yourself."

"You taught me about pleasure. Believe me, I'm not stupid enough not to pick my candidate well. In fact, I think I'll ask for Pippa's help. She's got to know some men with your experience who would make it good for me." If she hadn't been so angry, so frustrated, she would never have considered this course.

He groaned deep in his throat, the enraged roar of the male animal pushed too hard and too far. "Over my dead body and yours, too," he muttered, swinging her up and over his shoulder.

Christiana started struggling the second her feet left the floor. The look in Rich's eyes was heart-stopping and yet a part of her was filled with a sense of power for having forced his hand. "I don't need to be carried. I can walk," she mumbled, wiggling. "I feel like a slave woman in this position." A second later she grasped as a hard hand stung her bottom.

"If you can manage to shut up until we get some privacy, I might just cool down enough not to shake your brains back in order," Rich said roughly, reaching the top of the stairs.

"Good move," Josh murmured as he and Pippa came out of their room in time to hear the last. He glanced at his wife, smiling wickedly. "I wish I had thought to use it on you."

Pippa grinned naughtily. "Want to go downstairs and give it a shot?"

Christiana braced her hand on Rich's belt. With the other hand, she brushed her hair out of her eyes. She raised her head to glare at the older couple. "You could help me, you know."

Pippa shook her head, chuckling. "Told you. I only introduce. I don't interfere. You're on your own."

Josh snorted rudely.

Pippa evened the score with a very unwifelike elbow in his ribs. "Besides, my Masarati is getting closer all the time."

"Will you quit referring to that stupid bet?" Christiana snapped, forgetting her cool and who she was talking to. What little dignity she had was shot. "Rich, so help me if you don't let me down . . ." Another smack landed on her rear.

"She's getting testy. I'd better get on with my work."

"Work!" Christiana wailed irately.

"Work?" Pippa looked at her husband. "I thought you said he was good with women."

Josh shrugged, ignoring his friend's nasty look. "Well, I thought he was, and since I'm not ever going to be on the receiving end, how could I know for sure?"

Rich didn't wait for any more insults. He pushed past the pair without another word.

"Dinner is in an hour, or would you rather raid the refrigerator later?" Pippa called to Christiana.

"Just leave a knife in easy reach and forget the meal. I promise you I won't be hungry for food."

"That's the first correct thing you've said since I got home," Rich muttered, thrusting open his door and then slamming it behind them. He crossed to the bed and dumped Christiana in the middle, grabbing her leg when she tried to slide off the other side. "Don't bother running. That door has an automatic lock. By the time you get it open I'll have you again."

Christiana blew her hair out of her eyes and rose on her knees to face him. "I won't let you do this."

Rich stripped off his shirt without taking his eyes from hers. "You made the rules. I'm simply playing the game. Don't worry. You will get more pleasure than you know what to do with."

ELEVEN

Christiana watched his purposeful moves, seeing that she had driven him over the edge. For a moment she quailed at the prospect of making love with him in this mood. But she could think of no other way to make him realize what he was doing to them. "Is this what you really want for us?" she asked, facing him and demanding he confront himself. "To come together without the kind of emotion that we both are capable of?"

Rich dropped the last of his clothes on the floor, then looked at her kneeling there. The acceptance in those calm, clear eyes made him hesitate. He didn't want the loving between them to ever be driven by anger, by a need to hurt and yet he couldn't forget what she had said. "I have never felt this much emotion in my life. I told you what I could give. You'll have all of that. I can't do more, no matter how much I might want to. But I will not let you go to another man for spite." He took a step closer, holding her gaze, fighting his need to lash back, to hurt her as she was hurting him. "I warned you. Why didn't you listen?"

Christiána was suddenly tired of the tricks, the strategy and struggling. Truth was all she had left and all she wanted between them. "I'm fighting for my life," she said simply, lifting her empty hands and looking at them. "I need you to fill me and the future. Instead of holding nothing when I'm without you."

Rich stared at the vulnerable curve of her neck, the bowed head, the soft voice that held no hope only acceptance of the moments beyond the present. Sighing, he felt his anger drain away, leaving only the love that hadn't been strong enough in the past to last forever. His fingers shaking slightly, he lifted her chin, cupping her cheek. If only he could have come to her without any memories. "How do I fight you? It was hard enough fighting myself."

Her hand covered his as she leaned into the gentle caress. "Don't fight either of us. There is no need. I promise. I understand why you won't legally commit yourself to me. I don't agree. But I won't walk away. All I'm asking is that you stop chaining us both to your past. I'm not those women."

"But I'm still that man."

She smiled then, a sad curve of her lips. "You aren't. But until you know that, whatever we build together will be flawed."

"You'd take me like that?" Rich stared at her, trying to accept her choice and the kind of strength it had taken.

"I must."

He groaned, feeling something without a name

deep in his soul start to crack. He drew her to him, needing to hide her face so that he could not see her sacrifice. "I should send you away, but I'm not unselfish enough to do it."

Christiana's hands slipped over the smooth muscles of his back, kneading the tight flesh. She breathed in his scent, praying that she had chosen the right path. Her own destruction lay in the future if she had judged him more than he was. A quiver slipped through her and she pressed closer, no more eager than he to look in his eyes. To cover her reaction, she whispered, "Our hour is ticking."

He laid his cheek on her hair, for one moment giving in to the need to just hold her. "I know."

She pressed her lips to his nipples, licking at the taut peaks. His groan and the sudden tightening of his hands broke the closeness of the moment.

"Don't tease me. I want you too much to be gentle this time."

She lifted her head then. "I'm not glass. I won't shatter in your hands." She touched his face, stroking the clearly defined jawline. "I want you however you are."

The fierce need to possess died. Savoring his treasure offered more joy, more fulfillment. "Woman, you unman me with your honesty," he whispered as he slipped the blouse off her shoulders, pausing to trail a line of kisses over her soft skin. He blew gently on her neck. "You like that, do you?" he murmured as she shivered in pleasure. "How about this?" His tongue traced the line of the top of her bra, darting under the edge of the lace in tantalizing forays toward the peaks of her breasts.

Christiana's eyes drifted shut, her head feeling too

heavy to be held aloft. Her neck bent back over his arm as his mouth settled in the hollow between her breasts. When he released the front closure of her bra she felt the brush of cool air over her heated flesh. She pressed closer to his warmth.

"You taste delicious. Clean, sweet, and all woman," he whispered against her throat. He eased her back on the bed, coming down beside her in a smooth move without taking his arms away. His hand settled on her stomach, kneading the soft curve in slowly expanding circles.

Christiana responded to the easy caress, her legs shifting restlessly on the coverlet. Forcing her heavy lashes open, she focused on him. She wanted to say something, do something to tell him how much he was pleasing her and yet all she could do was look at him, drinking in the expression of pure pleasure on his face as one would thirst after water in the desert. "Rich." His name emerged as a muted whisper.

He bent, taking her lips, tasting his name, giving her own back. His fingers slipped beneath the elastic waist of her skirt. Her soft moan tore at his control. "Easy, pretty woman. It has been a long time since I held you. My dreams were not even close." His hand slipped lower, tracing the outline of her brief panties, teasing the silk as he would soon tease the flesh it covered.

"I can't take this," Christiana breathed, feeling as though she were catching fire from the inside out. Her nails dug into his shoulders as she arched toward him.

Rich pushed the skirt over her hips, sliding it down her legs in a quick pass. He gazed at his prize, his woman, his lover. Only a scrap of pink fabric and lace remained between them. Oddly, he found that instead of resenting its presence, the feminine wisp pleased him greatly. He touched the delicate garment, fascinated by the way it clung to her shape, cupping her, stroking the line of her hips to dip out of sight between her legs.

Christiana felt his eyes pass over her as though she were the most beautiful creature on earth.

"If I had looked a million years and a day, I could not have found someone who mattered to me as much as you," Rich said, raising his head to meet her eyes. "Whatever happens in the future I want you to remember that, this night and this moment. When I make you mine, when I give myself to you, there is no flaw in us. In me, yes. But not in you. Not in us." He touched her lips with his. "Do you believe me?" he whispered.

Christiana wanted to cry at the naked need showing so clearly in his eyes. She knew without knowing how she knew that if she answered in the negative, no power, no trick, no threat would make him let her stay. "Yes," she murmured, loving him then with more strength than she had known herself capable. She reached down and wiggled out of her panties, kicking them off. Winding her arms around his shoulders, she pulled him down to her. "Come into me. I want you."

Rich buried his face in her shoulder as he settled against her, letting her feel his weight. Her scent was everywhere, calling to him, invisible strands of memory that would forever haunt him. Even as his hands moved over her willing body, his mind was reaching out to her, whispering needs and hopes that he had shared with no other woman. Passion came in a rush which neither of them fought. Nothing was held back as Rich joined them in one quick stroke. Her soft cries of passion, the woman-rich fragrance, and the quick movements of her slender body crowded out the pictures of the past, writing a new history.

Tension spiraled between them. He drove into her, marveling at the way she returned his power, demanding more. She was strong, his mate. Suddenly the summit loomed before them. Christiana felt her body gather within itself. Her breath came in swift gasps, her hands seemed to know Rich's body as well as they knew her own. She arched into him, racing him for the finish. His hoarse voice in her ear, the hot flesh branding her own, was the last push she needed to reach the top. Suddenly she felt the world falling away beneath her back, darkness hovered, trying to trap her in its seamless folds. She stiffened, crying out his name. His arms caught her so close, breathing seemed impossible.

"Hold on, I'm with you," Rich commanded hoarsely. "Now!"

Christiana stiffened for a split second, then heat rushed through her, softening her muscles, flooding her thoughts. And she was falling. But not alone. Rich was there, holding her, keeping her safe. Her lashes shut because she no longer had the strength to keep them open. Silence encircled her so that the only reality was Rich and being held in his arms. It could have been moments or hours later when she opened her eyes to find him watching her. She tried to smile but found even that effort seemed beyond her.

"I didn't think it would be like this each time," she whispered, stunned at how soft and insubstantial her voice sounded.

He smiled gently as he touched her lips, tracing the fullness that was still swollen from his kisses. "For us I think it always will be. You're a rare and beautiful creature, Christiana Drake. You give so much and make me need to give so much in return."

He kissed her deeply, inhaling that special fragrance that was uniquely hers. "But right now all I want is you in my arms and a pillow beneath my head."

She sighed pleasurably. "Let's. The twins are asleep for the night and we aren't expected at the dinner table."

"It's not very romantic."

She pulled him down, touched when he laid his head on her breast, and wrapped his arms around her, pulling her closer still. "I think it's exactly what I need right now. Besides, we'll make our own rules of romance."

He chuckled softly. "If you wake up before I do, don't go without letting me know."

"I won't," she promised staring into the darkness, silvered visible by the moonlight pouring through the windows. She listened to his breathing slow as sleep crept over him, knowing that rest for her would be a long time in coming. But it didn't matter. Holding him and lying with him gave her more than sleep ever could.

"How is the plan coming?" Kay glanced at her cousin and then quickly away. His eyes saw too much.

"I've found the team to take the nanny and the twins."

She fidgeted with the bracelet on her wrist. "Good. When?"

In contrast, Nick was totally calm, in control. "Now that depends on the woman's schedule. It doesn't seem to be very reliable. I've got the team split into two parts, ostensibly fishermen working the river. They will be taking turns so that one boat won't be sitting off shore day after day. We don't want anyone getting suspicious."

"I wish this were over. I feel like someone is watching me every time I leave here. You promised me that taking that formula wouldn't be too difficult."

"The guard we bribed wouldn't have talked if you hadn't decided to get sticky fingers and try to skim some of the payoff," he reminded her brutally.

"I explained about that. I needed that money to pay off my debt."

"That gambling is going to get you killed, you fool. You're lucky I didn't do it myself."

She turned away from him, frightened. "I haven't been near the track. Just like I promised." She held out her hands, their shaking clearly visible even across the room. "I'm living on my nerves. I need the high that I get from there, but I haven't gone."

"And you won't."

She looked at him. Slowly she nodded, knowing that she had gotten the only second chance he would allow.

Nick tossed a packet of money to her. "Take this and go to the address written on the envelope. The guy there is expecting you. Don't mess up this time. I won't forgive you twice."

*   *   *

Rich rolled on his side, his hands sliding gently over Christiana's length. Her face, in sleep, was as calm and serene as always. He visually traced her features, smiling as her lips curved in her dreams. He dipped his head, unable to resist the taste of that smile.

Christiana felt his mouth settle on hers. Sleep slipped lightly into consciousness. Her arms lifted, gliding around his shoulders. She tilted her head back as he trailed kisses down her throat. Her body recognized its lover. "Again?" she whispered throatily as he teased her breasts with moist darts of his tongue.

"I'm discovering I'm insatiable where you're concerned." He raised his head, his eyes gleaming devilishly. "Do you mind?"

She laughed softly, her fingers dancing over his chest, tripping through the sprinkling of hair arrowing down to his waist. His bitten-off gasp of pleasure at her touch pleased her. "Does it feel as though I do?" she murmured, rotating her hips so that every part of his body felt hers.

Rich slipped his arms beneath her, then rolled smoothly onto his back, bringing her astride him. He looked up at her, grinning at her startled expression. "Bet you thought I didn't have anything new to show you."

"Well, now that you mention it. Last night was a very extensive course."

He frowned slightly, searching her eyes. "Much as I want you, my love, maybe we had better save this, delicious though it is. I don't want you sore. You are still new at this and every time I get within range I tend to think in marathons."

Laughing softly, she bent her head, kissing him, finding yet another facet to add to their love. "Not a chance. I ache a little, but it feels good. And no one, not even you, is going to keep us apart."

He slid his hands under her hair, holding her head, looking into those bright eyes that seemed to see all the way to his soul. The image she had of him was so shiny he felt humbled. "Woman, I wish there were words to tell you how much I love you." Regret for the women in his past had never been stronger. If only he could have come to her as fresh as she had come to him.

Although she could read his thoughts as clearly as though he had spoken, Christiana smiled anyway, tracing his lips with her forefinger. Whatever the cost, this man was worth the price and the wait. "Then show me," she whispered before easing down his body to join them as one.

"Well, little man, let's get you ready for a bit of a walk. Don't squirm like that. Lori's already set." Christiana pulled on the bright-blue sun suit, smiling at J. Jr.'s attempts to avoid being thrust into clothing. Even as her mind focused on the physical activity of the children's schedule, Christiana remembered the hours over the past three nights spent in Rich's bed. Every time she moved, her newly sensitized body reminded her of all that it was learning. Pleasure, delight, giving, passion. Words, emotions, sensations without end. Rich. His name, his being, were the summation of all of them. Her lips curved gently, her eyes sad yet hopeful, too. He was weakening. She could feel it. Her hope had not been in vain. It would take time. But they had time. She looked down at J. Jr. One day, if she were very lucky, maybe there would be a miniature of her or Rich to hold in her arms.

"River, now?" J. Jr. wiggled loose and headed for the door.

Christiana shook her head, smiling at the child's eagerness, thoughts of Rich and their desire slipping into the corner of her mind where all her treasured memories lay. She caught Lori's hand, just managing to snag J. Jr. before he escaped. "I swear, you're going to beat me one day," she mumbled, keeping a close eye on the more adventurous of her charges.

He grinned up at her, his expression gleefully agreeing. Christiana couldn't help but grin back. As they slipped out the back of the house, she released J. Jr.'s hand, knowing that in one thing he could be trusted. He would stay on the path that would take them to the dock at the river's edge. Although keeping J. Jr. in sight, she and Lori followed at a slower pace. Automatically, Christiana also kept an eye on her surroundings. The years of working as a bodyguard as well as a nanny for children had created habits that would never die. A frown marred her brow as she spotted the boat lying off shore again this morning. This was the third day she had noticed one working this part of the river. After yesterday's appearance, despite the fact the boat was a different one but anchored in exactly the same place, she had mentioned the situation to Josh, believing the craft to be part of the normal group of boats that frequented the river but not prepared to take the chance. Josh had been reassuring but equally as careful as she, promising to check the registration out as well as increasing the guard on the river side of the estate.

Thinking of the guard, Christiana glanced around, her mood changing as she realized that he was nowhere in sight. She glanced at her watch. They were early, but still . . .

She looked back to the river, feeling a stirring of instinct that demanded she inspect the scene more closely. Today, the craft, the same as the first day, was only a few yards from the beach. Her gaze focused on the fishing rods sticking up in the aft section. Why was it that they didn't look right? she wondered uneasily.

"J.'s getting ahead of us, Lori. Let's do a little trot to the pier," she suggested, quickening her step. The little girl giggled, thinking it a game. Even as she spoke, Christiana was scanning the water. If asked, she couldn't have said what she was looking for, but the moment she spotted the bubbles cutting a straight path toward them, she stiffened. "J. Jr.," she shouted. "Come here now!" The boy was never one to obey immediately. Knowing she could save at least one twin if she acted quickly, Christiana made a split-second decision.

Stopping, she pulled Lori around to face her. "Lori, go to the house. Get your mother," she commanded urgently. "I need her." She turned the child in the direction of the house, giving her a gentle push to emphasize the command. "Hurry, Lori, it's important."

The minute she was certain Lori would do as she was told, Christiana raced for the dock. She was still yards away from J. Jr. when the first diver emerged and came ashore. The black-garbed figure had spotted her. A second figure came out of the water, stripping his tanks and flippers with the same haste as the first.

"Damn," Christiana muttered, putting on an extra burst of speed that took her to J. Jr.'s side before the men reached the child. Without time for gentleness, Christiana grabbed his arm and all but threw him behind her and against the small shed that stood at the end of the dock. Two against one were not good odds, especially when she couldn't count on J. Jr. to stay put.

"Want a fight, do you, lady?" The first of the two men closed on Christiana's right.

Christiana divided her gaze between the pair. "Stay down, J. Jr.," she commanded grittily, sinking into a defensive stance.

"You're wasting your time, honey. You won't beat us both," the second man said roughly.

Even before he finished speaking, the first dove for her. Christiana caught him in the chest with a kick. He fell back with a grunt. J. Jr. shouted gleefully behind her. The second came straight on the heels of the other attack. Christiana parried a blow aimed at her head with a block then a right hand strike. The man cursed and swung again. She caught the first man moving out of the corner of her eye. Grabbing the second, she got ready to fling him at his partner. At that moment, J. Jr. scooted from behind her straight into the arms of the larger man. His scream of outrage was cut off abruptly with a cruel arm thrust around his tiny neck.

"Let him go, lady, or the kid's going to be hurting."

Christiana stared into the dark eyes glaring at her and knew he wasn't bluffing. Suddenly a woman's shout caught their attention. Christiana had an instant of consciousness to see Pippa racing toward them with murder in her eyes, just before her prisoner clipped her behind the ear. Then pain exploded, sounding like a car being overrevved in her brain. She didn't feel her body being slung over her assailant's shoulder. She didn't even grunt when she was thrown into the boat that had slammed into the beach only a few feet from their position. She didn't hear J. Jr.'s scream for his mother or see the anguish on Pippa's face as the boat reversed at full throttle and powered away.

"Pippa!" Josh roared, hurrying through the front door on the run. "Where are you?" His face tight with anxiety and fear, Josh strode toward the stairs, again shouting for his wife. He and Rich had been on their way to the office when Pippa's call had caught them. Wasting no time, he had ordered the limo to return to the house, every second more precious than his next breath.

Rich followed close on his heels, rage at the thought of Christiana in danger doing a war dance in his brain. Since he had received the news, the only thing that had kept him in control was the knowledge that he and Josh were her only chance to come out of this unharmed. His fists flexed in reaction as he slammed the door behind them.

"I'm here, Josh," Pippa said, coming out of the study. She couldn't seem to stop shaking, the image of her son crying for her indelibly etched in her thoughts.

Josh did an abrupt right turn, snatching his wife off her feet and against his chest all in one motion.

"Damn it to hell," Josh swore roughly, holding her tight. "Any word?"

Pippa stifled the need to howl her eyes out against his shoulder. "No," she whispered brokenly, then forced her voice and body to steady. She had to think. Her child's life and that of Christiana depended on all of them keeping their heads. "Just this." She pulled the carefully folded piece of paper the last man to board the getaway boat had tossed on the ground.

Josh kept one arm around Pippa's waist as he flipped the paper open and read aloud. " 'One call to the police and we'll kill the kids and the woman. Your lines are monitored. Wait for word.' "

Rich stared at the scrap of white in Josh's hand, feeling a fresh surge of rage at the threat. Pippa's sketchy tale of Christiana's attempt to save J. Jr. and the blow she had taken in the end was corrosive acid in his thoughts. Hearing how she had been manhandled had pushed him past the point of reasoning. His one instinct was to save his woman and the child she had risked her life to protect. He didn't care what he had to do or how he had to do it, but Christiana would be safe or he would forfeit his own life in the struggle to free her. None of his thoughts showed on his face as he looked up from the note that was their only link with the kidnappers. Pippa and Josh had their own pain. He would not make theirs worse.

His voice was as smooth as a polished diamond as he spoke. "It says *kids*. They figured to get them both." He met Josh's eyes, then glanced at Pippa. "Christiana saved one of them."

Pippa touched his arm, her pain deep, but her thought for him real. "I know. She was wonderful.

If J. Jr . . .'' Her voice shattered on his name then fused to finish. "Hadn't run when he did, they might be here now."

"No one blames him. No matter what happens, no one will." He looked at Josh, knowing the pair needed time alone, while he needed action to blunt the edge of his temper. Clear thought, not emotion, would save Christiana and J. Jr. "I'll check the grounds and the guards. The dogs should have picked up the intruders even if the men weren't fast enough." If there was a traitor in the compound he wanted the culprit found. It was a slim chance for a lead, but the situation was desperate. Any clue was more than they had now.

His arm around Pippa, Josh inclined his head. "We'll get them. Both of them. Christiana matters to us, too."

"They hit her." Rich gritted his teeth even as he said the words.

Pippa winced, remembering the attack. "It won't help much, but it wasn't a clumsy blow. They only seemed to want her out, not hurt. They must know they need her to handle J. Jr."

"Dutch comfort. A four-year-old kid can't be counted on to give an accurate description. But a full-grown woman with Christiana's background can. And she's expendable."

"Not to us," Josh denied immediately, the same idea in his mind. "That was our son she tried to save and our daughter she did protect. We'll get her back for you."

"Whatever happens, they'll pay for this. And that's a promise." With that vow, Rich turned and left the room.

"I've never seen him like that. There isn't a sign of distress on his face, but I can feel his rage as though he were shouting it." Pippa touched Josh's face, his anxiety clear.

"They have his woman. I know how I'd feel if it were you. And I know how I do feel knowing that J. Jr. is in their hands. There isn't a place anyone in this will be able to hide. There isn't anything I won't do to get our son back." Josh looked down at her, the same turbulence and deadly purpose that Rich was feeling reflected in his eyes. "Rich will have to stand in line if I get to them first."

Pippa pressed her fingers to his lips. "Get them back. Whatever it takes, get them back. Then I'll hold them still for both of you if that's what you want."

Josh bent his head, kissing her hard. "I'll get them for you, wife," he murmured, giving his own word.

Rich strode through the door of the study, his movements quick, tense, but completely controlled. "At least the riddle of the damn dogs is solved. They were drugged. The front guard found them both over by the west wall, along with the guard that was supposed to be at the dock. Looks like an air-powered dart gun did the job. Kay, wherever she is, has a lot to answer for." Rich flung himself into the chair beside Josh's desk. He glanced around. "Where's Pippa?"

Josh exhaled deeply, leaning back in his seat. He, like Rich, had accepted the fact that Rich's ex-wife was involved in the plot against them. "She's with Lori trying to get her calm enough to take a nap. Elsa is seeing to lunch."

"I'm not hungry."

"Neither are the rest of us. But we all will eat. Then we'll wait. Until we know exactly where and when they want the prototypes delivered, we wait."

"I don't like doing nothing."

"Do you think I do? That's my son, damn it," Josh bit out shortly.

Rich grimaced. "I didn't forget. I just can't get Pippa's account out of my mind. That creep threw her in the boat. There is no telling what kind of damage that did."

"Christiana is no ordinary woman. We all know that. Have a little trust in her."

"She isn't superwoman, either," he shot back, remembering the soft skin that covered her glorious body, the slenderness of her limbs in spite of her splendid proportions. "She bleeds just like the rest of us."

"Damn it, Rich, will you shut up. I need to believe in your woman. Right now she's the only chance my son and she have."

TWELVE

Christiana moaned softly, feeling every bone in her body protest at the faint sound. With her lashes shut against the light coming from an unknown source, she feigned partial consciousness while she sorted her jumbled thoughts and impressions into working order. That she and J. Jr. had been kidnapped, she remembered too well for comfort. Her head felt as though someone were pounding on it with a sledgehammer. She hurt everywhere, dull throbbing aches that told of too many bruises. Fighting through the pain, she concentrated on the muscles, needing to know just how much of her motion was impaired. She wasn't tied, and from the sounds of the area around her, there was only one other person present, a fidgety person at that. Risking opening her eyes slightly, she scanned the room. Dark paneling and round windows too small to wiggle through were easy indicators of her immediate location. A boat. A large one, judging by the stability of the craft in the water. As her gaze traveled farther afield, she found another narrow bed similar to the one on which she lay. J. Jr. was there, tied hand and foot, his face white but otherwise unmarked. He was watching her as though his whole existence centered in her presence. Her lashes opened completely.

"Take it off." He shook his bound arm fretfully. "I'll be good."

Christiana eased into a vertical position, fighting the nausea of the blow and the rough handling she had evidently received after the fact. "Give me a minute," she whispered.

J. Jr. stared at her. "Are we playing?" he asked finally, confusion replacing some of the fear and restlessness.

Christiana moved carefully across the room, hoping whoever was guarding them from the outside was either far enough away that sound wouldn't carry or that the room was more insulated than it appeared. "Yes," she murmured, sitting down beside him. "This is a very hard game where you have to be extra quiet and do everything I tell you. I don't know if you're big enough to play." As expected, his expression firmed at the subtle dig at his youth. Christiana had learned early that this twin responded best to challenge.

"Am, too," he muttered fiercely, giving her a childishly lethal glare.

"You didn't earlier today," she reminded him sternly as she released his hands and feet.

"Didn't know we was playing," he protested, still keeping his voice down.

Christiana stole a quick glance at the door. "Okay.

We'll play. But you have to do everything I tell you," she repeated. "Promise?"

"Why?"

"Because we can't get to the castle without escaping from here, and I know the key to do that and you don't. Do you promise?"

Calm adult eyes met suspicious childish ones. Finally J. Jr. nodded. "Okay. But I'm boss when we get to the castle."

"Deal." Christiana held out her hand. One of J. Jr.'s favorite things was shaking hands like his father.

J. Jr. grinned, looking surprisingly like Pippa at her most diabolical. "Deal." He shook hard. "Now what?"

"I need information from my spy. You," she added when he looked confused.

A delighted expression danced across his face. "Okay, what ya want to know?"

"How many people were in the boat with us? Can you show me on your fingers?"

He puffed out his chest. "I counted," he replied indignantly. "Four on the little boat. Three on this one."

"Did the four come with us?"

He nodded. "'Had guns, too. Big ones. Like Cap'in Justice on the TV."

Christiana remembered the cartoon well and the Uzi the main character handled too vividly. It was one of the few shoot-'em-up types that the children were allowed to watch. Only the fact that the stories had strong right and wrong themes offset the more violent format. "What else did you see?"

"A woman. Skinny. Not pretty like Mommy or you. Yellow hair. Loud words."

"Did you hear any names?"

"Nick. Kay. Man outside is Hammer. He tied me up. Called me a brat." He leaned his head against Christiana's shoulder, for one moment affectionate in a way he rarely was. "Am I a brat?"

Christiana stroked the fair hair from his eyes, smiling. "No, but you are one little terror when you want to be."

He grinned, pleased with the tone and the description. Suddenly he sobered, his eyes lowering. "Hammer hurt you. You had 'em but the other grabbed me when I ran. I messed up."

J. Jr. was too quick to accept a lie. "You made a mistake. Things always happen when we make a mistake. But mistakes can be fixed. And we're going to fix this one together."

He looked up then. "I will listen this time. No matter what."

"Good. Now scoot over and let me get comfortable while we make our plans."

Kay glared at Nick, still remembering her fear on seeing Christiana's body brought abroad. She had thought the other woman was to be left at the estate. "I think bringing that damn woman along was a mistake. How are we going to keep her from identifying us? No one would believe the kid. But she's a witness."

"Shut up, Kay. This is my ball game now. The buyers want what they paid for yesterday. We don't have time to nurse that brat or your questionable sensibilities. You told me yourself he's impossible.

Let the woman keep him quiet for us. We'll get our little deal out of the way, drop the monster in his daddy's waiting arms and then let Hammer do his thing. Exit one woman and enter wealthy us.'' Nick eyed his cousin, watching her pale. "Nothing is going to go wrong. Luck won't risk his son by calling the police and nobody's going to care about the woman after it's all over. One more unsolved murder among the hundreds that happen every day. Big deal.''

Kay pushed her hands into the pockets of her slacks. "Murder?" she whispered. "She's sleeping with Rich. He isn't going to stop looking for us if something happens to her. He's like that.''

He laughed shortly. "Dog in the manger, my dear. I wouldn't have believed it if I hadn't seen it.''

She took three hasty steps toward him, her hands upraised to strike before she remembered the nature of the man she faced.

The amusement died in his face, his eyes suddenly as cold and empty as a tundra in midwinter. "I wouldn't. I'm no gentleman like your precious Richland. I hit back. A lot harder than I'm struck.''

"I hate you. I don't know why I ever let you talk me into this.''

"I didn't come up with this plan. You did. I didn't romance that guard, you did. Or forge your husband's signature to a letter of reference for me. You did. I didn't have the inside story on the household. You did. In fact, no one even knows I'm involved in this at all, except my men on this boat, also mine, and every one of them is totally loyal to the money I pay them. Blow this deal, baby, and you're the one taking the fall, not I. The worst that can be said is that I worked on the project in the beginning. There is no other connection. I saw to that.''

Kay froze, hating the truth almost as much as she hated him. But she had learned long ago when to fight and when to appear bowed by power. The latter choice was the most expedient and safest one now. ''All right. I get the message. But I don't have to like it.'' The last was added to allay any suspicions he might have.

Nick smiled, believing he had her under control once more. ''Read this,'' he commanded, handing her a piece of paper on which were printed the directions for the delivery of the ransom for the Luck twin.

''Joshua Luck will never agree to this,'' she said after she scanned the message.

''He'll agree when we send him a piece of the nanny as proof we mean business.''

Kay blanched, staring at him as though she had never seen him before.

''Of course, if you're very convincing, that kind of thing won't be necessary. Very messy, you know.''

Frightened as she had never been in her life, Kay nodded slowly. ''When do you want me to make the call?''

''Now.''

''From here?''

''Too easily traced. Jan will take you to a pay phone. And bring you back.'' He waited until she headed for the door. ''And he will listen while you read that, and only that.''

She turned quickly, startled at the hard note in his voice. ''You don't trust me?''

''No. I think you've got jelly for guts, my dear.

If I didn't need you for a front, you'd be preceding our little nanny into the hereafter." He waved her out. "Go. You have ninety minutes to complete the job or I'll send Hammer after you."

"I'm scared," J. Jr. whispered suddenly. "This is a funny kinda game. I wanna go home."

Christiana edged closer on the bed, giving him the comfort of her size and, she hoped, confidence in her authority and age. Had he been Lori she would have included a hug. "So do I, but we can't until we can get ourselves out of here."

"How?"

She looked him in the eye. "I don't know yet. But something will turn up if we watch for a clue."

"Like what?"

"Well, for starters, we need a key to open that lock."

"Hammer has it. I don't think he'll give it to us. He looks real mean."

The more Christiana heard of the as-yet-unseen Hammer, the less she thought their chances were of escape. With J. Jr. along there was just so much she could do, especially from a boat. Alone, she could easily swim to shore. J. Jr. couldn't. So, not only did they have to get out of here, but she had to find a getaway conveyance of some sort. Or wait for rescue. Until now she hadn't allowed herself to think of those left behind. Rich, Pippa, and Josh. What were they thinking? Doing? Had there been any clues? Was help on the way or were they as stymied as she? She shivered, feeling the licks of unwanted fear. She fought the emotion, determined to stay calm, to beat the odds. Without anyone telling her, she knew her role in this situation was an expendable one. She doubted their captors intended to harm J. Jr. at any point. But she was another matter. She could identify at least one of the kidnappers. Her death would be the only means to ensure her silence. Her lips twisted grimly. It was ironic, as life often was. Just when she had something and someone more to live for than her career, she was looking death in the face. At that moment the distinct sound of a key in the lock of the door scraped across her thoughts. She tensed, her attention focusing and sharpening as it opened. The panel eased back and she saw Hammer for the first time. If she ever wondered what real trouble looked like, she was staring right at it now.

"Okay, lady. Up. We're going for a little walk." He gestured her erect with one ham-sized hand.

Christiana unfolded her legs without hurrying, her mind working overtime. Being separated from J. Jr. wasn't a good sign for either of them. "Where?"

"Just walk. You'll find out when you get there."

"No," J. Jr. protested.

Christiana glanced at him, shaking her head. Hammer took a step toward the child. J. Jr. glared at him, but this time kept his promise to obey.

"Smart kid," the man growled, before catching hold of Christiana's arm and pushing her out the door, locking it behind him.

"I can't stand this," Pippa muttered, getting up and pacing the study. "Why don't they call?"

Josh clenched his hand around the glass of brandy he had been nursing for an hour. None of them had managed much lunch. "Strategy," he said flatly, controlled rage making his voice so even that nothing disturbed the slip of words.

Rich glanced up from the last of the report he had been rereading. "I still can't find anything in here to help us find her. Damn Kay for the edge she gave them."

"Neither of us really thought you would. It was just a chance anyway."

Pippa looked from one to the other, for once not really listening. "I couldn't care less about that now, unless you have the name of the monster who took my child," Pippa spit out, too angry to be controlled and too worried to be kind to a friend as anxious as she.

"I have one name all right. Just not the woman," Rich returned abruptly, guilty at the fact that it was because of him that Kay had ever come in contact with his friends and Christiana.

Josh placed his glass on the desk and rose to go to his wife. "We didn't want to make this any worse for you, darling, but Rich has turned up evidence that directly links Kay to this mess. We sent a team to her place days ago, but they found nothing. No forwarding address, no indication that she was ever returning to her apartment. Nor was there any indication of when she had left or with whom."

Pippa stared at him as though she couldn't believe he had withheld information. "Is that all?" she asked finally.

Josh touched her cheek. "Right or wrong, I love you. I can't help it if I would spare you."

She pressed his hand to her face, tears she would not shed standing in her eyes. "Don't do it anymore. Promise me."

"I won't." He pulled her into his arms. "God, I wish Joe were here. Maybe he could see what we can't." He tensed, glancing toward the door as it opened.

"I am here, Brother, but I'm not sure I can see anything," Joe said, walking into the room with Lyla at his side.

Josh released Pippa, hope flashing in his eyes as he saw his twin. "You're supposed to be in Palm Beach, working."

Lyla touched Pippa's arm, her eyes soft with concern. "He felt you both needed him. We had the pilot bring us back."

Rich rose, throwing the folder on the desk. Worry for the safety of J. Jr. and Christiana made mincemeat of his skepticism where Joe's paranormal abilities were concerned. At that moment he would have sold his soul to Satan in his red cape for a clue to bring his woman and the child home unharmed. "I don't much believe in the things that you do, Joe, but if you can help at all, I'll be the first one to say, go for it. Everything you have given us so far has been right on the money."

Joe looked at Rich. Before he could say anything, Josh spoke. "Can you help, Joe?" he asked.

"I honestly don't know. J. Jr.'s family. I'm not good in touching in on people that close. You know that."

Rich looked from one brother to the other, seeing the uncharacteristic defeat in Josh's eyes and the anguish in Joe's. Pippa's skin resembled milk, and even Lyla seemed lost. "Are you saying you won't do whatever it is you do?" he demanded.

"I'm saying, I'm too emotionally attached to

work as easily as I would like. What little I'm getting is a jumbled mess. It was like looking through murk just to pull out your ex-wife's name. I need something to focus on that isn't loaded with my personal feelings."

"Then go after it another way."

Four sets of eyes stared at him in varying stages of confusion.

"Meaning?" Josh asked the question on everyone's mind.

"Use me. I'm not kin to J. Jr. or Christiana." He spread his hands in a slicing arc of frustration and determination. "If you need a link, I'm it. I'm in love with Christiana and she is with me. Will that help?"

Josh took up the question. "Will it, Joe?"

Joe stared at Rich, reading the emotion blazing out of his eyes. "We'll damn well find out."

Suddenly the shrill ring of the phone broke the mood. The women froze, staring at the instrument.

"It's Kay," Joe said harshly before Josh could pick up the receiver.

Both Rich and Josh's curses hit the air at the same instant. Josh reached for the phone. Joe caught his hand. "There is a man with her, listening. Be careful what you say to her." The brothers' eyes met and held.

Josh inclined his head abruptly, his mouth a grim line as he lifted the receiver from its cradle. "Yes."

Kay swallowed hard at the sharp sound of Josh's voice. Paper in hand, she began to read, mindful of Jan standing at her shoulder. "You have until noon tomorrow to gather the plans, formulas, and models for the synthetic fuel and its burner. Precisely at twelve you will recieve one call with instructions for delivery. We are watching you and your plants in Tennessee and Arizona. Should the required information not be on its way to you by eight tonight, you will discover a small piece of your nanny delivered to your front gate at nine. It will be your only warning. Any other deviation will mean the body of your son." Kay was breathing hard when she hung up the phone and pushed past Jan to leave the booth.

Josh broke the connection, keeping his face calm with monumental effort. No matter what, he could not tell Pippa the gory details of the threats. "We have until noon tomorrow to get the plans, formulas, and models together for delivery. There will be one more call for final instructions. We make the drop, then J. Jr. and Christiana will be back with us."

Joe studied his brother. This time he didn't need his paranormal abilities to know what wasn't being said. He had been close enough to hear the information that Josh had so carefully edited. He glanced at his wife and Pippa. "I know this will be hard for you, but it will be clearer for me if I can work without either of you in the room."

Pippa nodded jerkily and took Lyla's arm. "Come on. Lori is probably awake now. You can help me keep her entertained."

The men watched the women leave the room, none of them speaking until the door closed behind them.

"What did you leave out?" Rich demanded sharply.

Josh sat down, feeling older than his years. Slowly, carefully, he related the call as close to verbatim as possible, trying not to see the sudden whitening of Rich's face or the spasmodic clenching of hands into fists. His curses echoed Josh's silent ones.

"I'm going to make the calls now. Get the stuff on the move. I don't want to find out whether they actually have anyone in a position to keep that kind of a watch."

Rich was past hearing Josh. All he could think about was Christiana and the danger in which she stood. Every instinct demanded he do something more than sit and try to reason through this. Logic and intelligence told him this was the only way. But his needs weren't logical and his fear had no intelligence. Both were blind to anything but his woman and their future.

"You did well, my dear," Nick purred, watching Kay move gracelessly toward him.

"I hate you," she hissed desperately, stopping at the bar to pour herself a drink. She downed it in one gulp, feeling the liquor begin to dispel the chill of the terror in her body. Her vision cleared, her body ceased its unrelenting trembling. When she finished the first shot, she poured another and sipped this time as she rotated to face her cousin. It was then she noticed Christiana's presence. "What's she doing here?" she demanded, staring into eyes too calm and analytical to belong to a woman soon to die.

"Meeting you."

"Why?"

"Every victim has a right to meet its destroyer."

Christiana watched the interplay, more interested in the moods and emotions than the actual words. The moment Hammer had shown her into this stateroom and she had confronted the mastermind of the plot, she knew her existence without intervention was limited. "So you're the one who will pull the trigger,'' she murmured, studying Kay. Nick had been amazingly forthcoming as to Kay's hand in the plot and her previous relationship to Rich. Rich had definitely picked more for looks than brains and bottom. If this female had any courage, it came out of the bottle she was holding like a lifeline.

Kay took a hasty step forward, then stopped at the cold, clear look in Christiana's eyes. ''This wasn't part of the plan,'' she sputtered at Nick.

He laughed. ''It passes the time.''

''It also leaves J. Jr. alone in that cabin. He is untied and he's not an obedient child,'' Christiana said, shrugging. She was taking a shot at the ego that had bought a vulgarly outfitted yacht. She wanted this man off balance if possible . . . and Kay more confused and frightened. Her tactics were long shots, but at least they were some kind of plan. ''Of course, with the money you're no doubt getting, you can afford to buy yourself a new boat if he wrecks this one.''

Nick glared. Kay choked on a laugh in midswallow. Nick signaled Hammer. ''Take the nanny back to her brat. Tie them up if she gives you any trouble.''

Christiana rose leisurely. Every nerve demanded action, but she forced her limbs to an easy pace. Every second she was outside, she was picking up more information. ''Do that and you'll have a problem for certain. J. Jr. has a good set of lungs. And gagging him will make him sick. Children are like that.'' She was stretching a point, but neither looked as if they knew anything about toddlers. ''Another thing. That cabin hasn't a bathroom. Unless you want to clean up a mess, you'd better have your man take us to one or put us somewhere else.''

Nick rose, his face darkening furiously. ''Nanny, you're asking for it. One more word and I won't wait until I don't need you anymore.''

Christiana shot a scornful look in Kay's direction. ''Intending to give J. Jr. over into her care. She'd jump ship or he would before you could return him to his parents.''

Nick glanced at Kay, forced into accepting that the woman was right. He didn't like the situation, but he could do nothing yet. ''I'm going to enjoy seeing you blown away.''

Christiana looked into his eyes and knew he meant every syllable. She said nothing. She still had some tricks and more prayers by the moment. She had to believe Rich was moving heaven and earth to get to her. And that Josh was holding back the tides and the seas to find J. Jr. Between them, one or all, they would escape. She had to believe that. Hers and J. Jr.'s lives depended on her faith.

_____ THIRTEEN _____

Joe moved to a chair near the fireplace. Lowering himself, he glanced at Josh. "Pull the drapes and disconnect the phone. Rich, lock the door, please."

Both men worked quickly to comply before joining in chairs close by.

"Now what?" Rich demanded impatiently.

Joe smiled grimly. "We all stay as calm and as quiet as possible and let me concentrate. I don't know how long this will take nor do I know what I will get. Your skepticism is going to be a fairly formidable barrier. You will help us all if you can clear your mind of as much of that as possible. Think of Christiana. What she means to you. Make her live in your thoughts. As you see her, so hopefully will I." He studied Rich, knowing how much he was asking, how hard it was going to be for Rich to relax enough for the images to come through clearly.

Rich scowled but said nothing.

Josh nodded at his brother, his face drawn with

worry and hope. "Do your best. That's all we're asking."

Joe looked at his twin, then closed his eyes. The truth was always easier to seek in darkness without the flash and brilliance of light to distract the searcher. Seconds dripped into minutes as he gently brought his thoughts to his nephew and the woman he had yet to meet. Even as he thought her name, he felt a surge of emotion coming from Rich. Confusion, love, fear, and rage splintered his focus, swirling in colors so vivid he could almost touch them. His body stiffened, fighting the intrusion, trying to obey the dictates of its owner.

Rich stared at Joe, seeing the sudden distress in the peace that had wreathed his features. Somehow he knew that his feelings were slipping from him to the other man. Startled, intrigued, he tried to push aside his need to understand, his demand for action to save the woman he loved, to create the environment Joe had said was required. Suddenly he, too, closed his eyes. Then she was there, wrapped in the glory of the dawn of their first meeting. He felt that first touch of desire, that awe of her skill and power. The next meeting came swiftly, the tangle of emotions and the lack of recognition. Even as it appeared, other more vivid scenes superimposed themselves on the screen of his thoughts. Their first kiss. The heat of passion. The moment of union. Memories, pages of history, hopes for the future. Then his fear spiraled out of the darkest corners to blot out the fire and the desire. He grabbed at the mental woman, needing her near to fight the eclipse of their tomorrows. She slipped from his grasp. Sweat beaded on his forehead as he fought to hold on.

Joe's soft but incisive voice snapped through the fog, sounding as though it were coming from inside his head rather than from beside him. "Stop fighting her. Let her lead us."

Shocked by the vocal intrusion, he lost the fight to keep Christiana as safe as he had last seen her. Then she was back, different now. There was a strange alteredness to her fine-honed body. Her eyes gleamed with the fire of primitive animal on the prowl. Even her voice sounded different. He frowned, knowing there was no way he could hear her. Nor see her. In that second he lost her, his eyes opening to the room he had almost forgotten existed. He stared at Joe, somehow unable to look away.

"She's on a boat, not far from here." Joe paused, searching for a name and finding none, although he could see the craft clearly. "White, red waterline stripe. Blue-green canvas and a small dingy trailing on the port side. They are all right. A game. Christiana's. Fear. Kay's. Nick." He hesitated, feeling the image beginning to fade.

Josh sat forward in his chair, wanting to know which direction. The St. John was a large river. He kept silent, aware of what the cost would be if he broke Joe's trance before the last drop of information was drained from it.

"Tomorrow there will be only one at the pick up." Joe opened his eyes, looking straight into Rich's. "Christiana won't be there. Just J. Jr."

Rich paled, the implications sliding like a knife to his heart. Her expendability had always been his fear. "Then we'll get them out tonight."

"We need a direction, Joe," Josh pointed out tersely.

"I wish I had one, but I don't."

"Then we split up and use boats to find the right craft," Rich said, already feeling the sands of Christiana's life dripping through his fingers.

They rose together. Joe touched both, a hand on each tense shoulder. "I may get more on the water. If I can get within range of them, I might be able to give us an edge."

Josh started to speak but Rich beat him to it. "You've given us more than we had. Whatever happens, you've given us a chance to get to them." Without another word, he shook off Joe's hand and went to the desk, dialing a number swiftly. He spoke tersely into the phone, then hung up. "In less than an hour, we'll have three high-speed boats and experienced drivers at your dock. Let's get it in gear."

" 'Ana, I don't like this game," J. Jr. whispered unhappily. "I want to go home." He leaned against her side, looking up at her.

Christiana cast a quick look over her shoulder to the closed door of the head. Beyond it, she could hear Hammer moving impatiently. "I know. But we have to play a while longer. Just until your daddy and Uncle Rich get here."

"You didn't tell me they were coming to play," he accused.

She went down on her knees beside him, catching his shoulders in her hands. "It's a surprise. But before they get here, you and I will have to get ready."

"How?"

"I want to get Hammer's gun."

The little boy screwed up his face, thinking. "How?"

"Tonight when he brings us our dinner, I want to pretend you're sick. Make a lot of noise. If you can, roll around on the cot like you're trying to get away from me." She touched his face, almost afraid of the chance she was taking but knowing no other way to even the odds. "I want you to hit me. Make it look really hard. I'm going to let go of you for a second. I want you to make a run for the door. But don't scream."

"OK."

"Come on, nanny. Hurry up in there," Hammer commanded, banging on the door.

"We're almost done," she called over her shoulder, and then turned back to J. Jr. urgently. "Stay away from the gun. Run past his other side. Can you do that for me?" She stared into his eyes.

He looked at her for an instant, suddenly older than four. "He'll try to catch me."

She nodded.

"You're gunna jump him?"

She nodded again.

"He's bigger than you. How do I help you?"

She smiled. "You will be doing the biggest job."

He grinned. "Yeah. Dad will be proud of me."

"All right, Josh," Slater McGuire agreed dryly, glancing sidelong at the man who wielded enough power to make him come at the first call. He ignored the other two men in the room. "I'll concede you didn't want the locals in on this kidnapping. I'll even concede you don't want the company on it, either. Their idea of a covert operation is fifteen guys in the field. Damn risky here. But what the devil do you expect to do, the three of you buzzing around out there? That's one of the heaviest patrolled pieces of water in this country. How are you planning to board that boat, assuming you do find it, of course, get the woman and your son secure and get off again? If what you tell me is true about that prototype synthetic fuel and the burner, you are playing for very high stakes. That doesn't argue a shoestring operation. And that snatch was no amateur job. Slick, real slick.''

Josh raked his hand through his hair, glaring at the man who could match him in control and cold nerve. They couldn't have been more different in looks, temperament, and aim in life, and yet they were, had been since the moment of meeting, fifteen years before, friends. "Don't be any more stupid than you can help," he shot back roughly. "That's why you're here. Joe has given us a lead. Rich has three top drivers and boats on the way here right now. You're going to help us plan this operation and get those damn contacts of yours to clean up the mess when we're through.''

Slater stared at him, for once shaken out of his cynical regard of humankind by the blunt announcement. It had been nine years since anyone had had the nerve to order him around. He had never taken commands well. "You're pushing it.''

"Give me a better idea then. As you so rightly pointed out the moment you walked through the door, we're amateurs. You're a pro. You direct. We do. We've got one shot to make this work. Two lives depend on us getting it right.''

"You're crazy. Those are real guns out there.''

"With the people we love," Rich added harshly, speaking for the first time. "Either you show us how to get in there and get them out or we do it on our own.''

Slater shot Rich a look of acute dislike. "I don't like you, Rich man. You think you can buy anything.''

"And you've got a chip on your shoulder about being brought up in the back of a truck. Big deal. You can try to punch my face in when this is over. Right now, your knowledge and our manpower and determination are the only things Christiana and J. Jr. have going for them.''

"The nanny's your woman.''

"That's none of your business.''

The two squared off. Big men, almost the same height, long of limb, tough of mind, neither was prepared to budge from his position.

"This will get us nowhere.'' Joe rose to step between the two. "I'll referee if that's what you want when this is over. Right now let's get going. The boats are here.''

At that moment, the sound of high-powered engines reached the room. The other three turned to the windows.

"Joe, you still give me the creeps with that ability of yours,'' Slater grunted, going to the window to eye the sleek, deep-bottomed craft idling at the dock. "All right. I'll help you. But if any of you value your tails, don't get trigger happy. Cleaning up the wounded is a hell of a lot easier if I don't have to explain dead bodies draped around in your wake. I'll go with Josh when we split up to search. Whoever sights them, identify the craft then get back here. Watch what you say on the radio. They can hear us as easily as we can them. Just call in to the rest of us that you're having a problem with the engine.''

"We may be amateurs, but we're not stupid," Rich growled, following Josh and Slater out the study.

"You're asking for it, Rich man."

Rich stiffened, his frustration needing an outlet. The big male in front of him was the only available target. Only the knowledge that the rescue operation needed his knowledge and his contacts kept his hands at his sides and his smoldering temper in check.

Joe laid a hand on his shoulder. Rich glanced back, seeing the understanding in the psychic's eyes. He shook off the touch, turning from Slater to stride down the dock. There would be time enough later. He had to believe that.

"He's worried, too," Joe murmured as they separated to head for their boats.

Rich sighed deeply. "I know. That guy has always ridden me about my background. I'm a fool for letting it get to me now. Usually I can ignore him. He's got a temper like a rabid dog, but you have to admire his courage and his intelligence.''

Joe shook his head, smiling faintly. "And his timing is questionable.''

"Too bad someone doesn't point that out to him," Rich muttered before jumping into the craft he would use. He nodded to the driver and they surged away from the dock in a controlled roar. The other two boats followed quickly, rolling out at the prearranged site to begin the search. The day was fading fast, stealing the light that would increase their chances of success. Rich kept his eyes on the heavily populated waterway, scanning every vessel, trying to match the reality with Joe's vision.

Just as darkness fell, when Rich had passed the point of hope and settled into a grimly determined mode, the radio whipped out Joe's voice. "We've got engine trouble. We'll be going back to home base. Fifteen minutes." Rich released his breath in a rough oath as the boat swung in a wide arc back the way they had come. Their quarry had been spotted. It was time for action.

"Hang on, Christiana," he whispered below the roar of the engine.

Christiana glanced out the porthole, trying to judge how much of the day remained. For once in her life, waiting was a burden rather than an accepted fact. She looked over her shoulder to find J. Jr. watching her. "You haven't forgotten what you're supposed to do, have you?"

He gave her a disgusted stare. "No, I remember. And you keep asking me that."

"I know," she said turning back to the window. Rich's image seemed to dance on the gently undulating water. He was calling to her, silently sending her reassurance that she so desperately needed. Never having been one to lean on anyone in her life, it felt strange to need that image of the man and the comfort and pleasure she had found in his arms.

"Rich," she whispered, longing for his arms to take away the nightmare she was living. She was prepared to risk her life to save the child. She was prepared to face death if that was all that was left to her. But she wasn't prepared to know this need of his touch, this agony of loneliness and heart-ripping emptiness. Wrapping her arms around herself, she stared into the cloak of the night, remembering the passion and pleasure he had shown her. Remembering the joy and wonder she had found in his claiming. So much emotion, so much beauty. A legacy to hold the terror of these hours at bay. A promise of a future that might not come.

Suddenly the sound of the key in the lock tore through her thoughts. She turned quickly, looking to J. Jr. as she went to her bunk. The little boy, too, glanced at the door.

"I remember," he whispered just before the panel opened and Hammer's bulk filled what little space the cabin afforded.

"Move over with the kid, nanny," he ordered harshly, gesturing with the gun he held in his right hand.

Christiana obeyed, trying to look suitably meek and frightened. As soon as she was settled, their jailer spoke again.

"Keep the kid there while your food is brought in. One move from either of you and you go hungry for the night."

She nodded, making her movements jerky. His malicious smile told her the act had been bought. She watched closely as another man entered without glancing their way and placed a laden tray on the small table at the end of her cot and then left as quickly as he had come.

The next instant J. Jr. stiffened, contorting his face in a petulant lines. "I don't want to eat. I feel sick. I want to go home." He started to slide off the bunk.

Christiana caught him. Even she wasn't prepared for the way he erupted into a flurry of thwarted child.

Hands and feet seemed to pop up everywhere. She didn't have to fake a grunt of pain as one of his heels contacted with her ribs. Releasing him just enough for him to escape, she dropped back on the bunk. J. Jr. darted for the door. Hammer swore, making a grab for him. He missed and turned to try again.

Christiana lunged for Hammer, using both hands as a weapon against the back of his neck. He went down so suddenly she nearly toppled onto his prone body. "Get the door, J. Jr.," she commanded, slightly out of breath. Without looking up, she stripped the gun from Hammer's hand and checked the clip. Full.

"We did it," J. Jr. crowed, coming to her side and glaring down at their jailer. "Awesome."

Christiana ruffled his hair, a smile momentarily driving the gravity from her expression. "We're still trapped in here," she reminded him.

"You'll find a way out." He poked the man with his toe. "They tie this guy up on TV."

"And we will, too. We'll use my belt and his." It took a bit of grunting and pulling on her part and a lot of useless motions on J. Jr.'s, but they got Hammer trussed up like a holiday fowl without him coming to and stuffed him into the closet. As soon as Christiana was satisfied, she went to the door, easing it open to look up and down the corridor. It was empty. The only signs of life were sounds coming from the gallery area, a section they had to pass to get to the deck. Mentally cursing their location on the boat, she shut the door again. Hopefully no one would be paying attention to the fact that Hammer was among the missing.

*　*　*

"Set?" Rich asked tersely, glancing over to the other three men attired in the same black wet suits as he. Of the four of them he was the most experienced diver. Three nods responded to his question before they moved, one at a time, to the side of the boat and eased into the dark St. John's.

As the water closed over his head, Rich took the lead, mentally reviewing their plan of action. The yacht on which Christiana and J. Jr. were being held rode at anchor about a hundred yards away. The boat they had just left looked like many of the small pleasure crafts that populated the water in these hours. Two of the power boats were waiting about half a mile away. At a prearranged time, the pair would make a run at the yacht, swerving near to the starboard side, cutting too close to the craft. The noise of the high-powered motors plus the seeming recklessness of the drivers, would hopefully draw all eyes to starboard. The diversion would allow them to board port aft. With luck they could get below deck and locate Christiana without too much resistance. He hoped, he added silently as he led the group through the murky water, using his experience, a feel for distances, and a compass for guidance. A few moments later they surfaced silently beside the hull, stopping first at the anchor line to shed and secure their air tanks, flippers, and masks to the rope. Above him, Rich could see a man patrolling the deck, gun tucked with businesslike precision under his arm. He grimaced as he jerked a thumb upward in case the others hadn't seen him. No one risked speaking as sound carried easily at night. Rich glanced at his watch and, in that moment, he registered the steady roar of the power boats. Right on time. His body tightened, readying itself for the crucial instants of exposure. On board the yacht, the shouts of the men on guard came clearly, oaths drifting into the night as the diversion began. Josh pulled the rope with the grappling hook attached from his shoulder and tossed it over the railing. In seconds, Rich was out of the water and working his way to the gunwale, hand over hand. He dropped soundlessly to the deck, just as the power pair made another dive at the yacht. Joe was next on board, then Josh, and finally Slater.

"I've got the point," Rich whispered.

"I'll keep watch up here with Joe," Slater added, his eyes scanning the area.

Rich nodded once, before leading the way to the hatch to the interior of the boat.

"What's happening?" J. Jr. demanded, hopping up and down, trying to see out the porthole where Christiana stood.

The noise from the high-powered engines outside sounded like a swarm of angry bees. "Two boats are making runs at us," she murmured absently, watching the synchronized aquatic maneuver. "I think we're about to have company," she added, turning from the small window and getting a good grip on her gun. She spared a glance for the closet that housed Hammer. No sound emerged so it was safe to assume he was still enjoying his unearned rest. "Get under that bunk and stay there unless I call you." She pushed J. Jr. into the only reasonably unnoticeable hiding place left in the cabin. "No matter what you hear, don't come out unless I call you, J. Jr. That's our code that it's all right to come out.''

''I want to help.''

''No.'' She slipped his head firmly under the spread. ''There's only one gun. Help me by hiding. They'll be so busy looking for you that I'll be able to get them just like we got Hammer.''

''OK. But you're getting all the good stuff,'' he mumbled, his voice muffled by the fabric curtain.

Christiana's face tightened into grim lines as she stared at the door, the gun poised to do the most damage in the least amount of time. If it was as she thought—a rescue operation—one of the kidnappers might just decide to use J. Jr. as a bargaining tool. That was one price she intended to make too high for them to want to pay.

''Where are they?'' Rich growled under his breath as they opened the second door without finding anyone. Josh nudged him from behind just as one man came out of the galley practically on top of them. With no time or room to maneuver, Rich drove the butt of his gun into the man's stomach. He folded like a deflated balloon. Josh reached past him to grab the body before it noisily hit the floor.

''One down,'' he murmured, stripping him of his weapon, a small handgun.

Rich ignored the comment to ease into the galley. It was deserted.

''Let's stash him in the food locker,'' Josh suggested, yanking the comatose man into the room by his collar. Without waiting for an agreement, he locked up his prisoner.

Rich kept guard at the door. The commotion going

on outside was making more noise than they had hoped. But it couldn't continue before someone got wise. "Let's split."

"I was thinking the same thing myself."

They moved back into the corridor, each taking one side, alternately opening doors.

Christiana could hear the methodical search. Everything in her said that help was in the hall, but with J. Jr. behind her she didn't dare take the chance of finding out. So she waited, her finger on the trigger. She had no illusions. If it wasn't help out there, she had little time to even the odds before someone got to her. And with her gone, J. Jr. wouldn't stand a chance.

Suddenly they were there. Her eyes focused on the knob as it turned quickly. She inhaled, holding her breath. The door swung open. Her hand tightened.

Rich stared down the muzzle of the gun and the clear-eyed woman holding it aimed at his belly. "Shoot me later, woman. Right now let's get you and J. Jr. out of here," he said roughly, just managing to keep himself from yanking her into his arms. Relief coursed through him at her smile.

Christiana laughed softly as her hand relaxed. "J. Jr., let's go," she called, moving toward Rich, needing to touch him just for an instant.

J. Jr. popped out from under the bunk just as Josh pushed past Rich into the room. J. Jr. hurled into his father's waiting arms. Rich allowed himself one deep, rough kiss, which was fully returned before he set his woman from him. "Hold that thought," he commanded, edging back into the corridor. "Follow me and keep J. Jr. behind you. Josh will get the rear."

"Lead on," Christiana said, ready to meet anything if it meant getting J. Jr. to safety.

Suddenly gunfire erupted on deck. Josh and Rich swore an oath that drew a comment from J. Jr. Josh hushed him impatiently.

"I knew it was too good to last," Josh muttered just as two men hurried through the door from the salon only to stop as though yanked by a single string at the sight of three weapons trained on them.

"Drops the guns." Rich waited while they complied, then added harshly, "Move it." He gestured them back the way they had come.

Kay turned as the group filled the salon. Drink in hand, her mouth agape at the intrusion, she froze. Silence came swiftly. Then out of the darkness and lack of life came two voices, Slater and Joe's. Curses, Slater's and amusement, Joe's. Rich and Christiana exchanged glances as Josh put his hand on his son's shoulder.

"Rich," Kay said finally, faintly, drawing everyone's attention.

Rich glared at his ex-wife. "In the flesh and mad as hell." His hand sliced in an angry arc. "Get on that couch and stay there before I forget men aren't supposed to use brutality on women."

"Don't worry about it, darling. She moves and she's mine," Christiana murmured, staring at the other woman. She had her own score to settle with the blonde. "By the way, you're right. You do have the worst taste in women."

He grinned at her. "Until you."

She laughed, her eyes gleaming with the relief of knowing the nightmare was over and Rich was by her side. "Well, even idiots occasionally hit it lucky."

Josh finished settling their captives into chairs in the corner and chuckled at the comment. "Rich, you are definitely in trouble."

Joe pushed a wounded man into the salon. "But Christiana is good at handling trouble," he pointed out, taking in the scene at a glance.

Slater was right on his heels. "I'll second that even if I don't like the circumstances." He propped a hip on the table and surveyed the captives. "This it?"

"One in the food locker," Josh added.

"I left one tied up in the forward cabin," Christiana admitted, noting Rich's sharp look. "Well, how did you think I came by this?" She nodded toward the gun in her hand. "They didn't give it to me because of my body."

"We'll talk about your body and your propensity for landing yourself in trouble when we get home," he murmured, trading her glance for glance.

"What about my cousin?" Kay asked, staring at Slater. "He went out to help the men."

Slater's face was grim. "This and the other two are it."

Kay paled even more, her skin the color of skim milk. Had she not put J. Jr.'s life on the line, Christiana could have felt pity for the older woman in that moment.

"Rich, I never meant for it to turn out this way. Nick told me no one would be hurt. I didn't know he meant to kill her. All we were doing was trying to get hold of the plans for the burner and the formula for the fuel. You would have gotten the kid back, I swear."

Rich stared at the woman he had once thought he

loved. As he looked at what she had become, he felt the last lingering traces of the ties with the past slip free. "Kidnapping is a federal crime. Slater here is the man you should talk to."

"He doesn't know me. He doesn't care." She rose, her hands outstretched, her eyes pleading for mercy, her voice quivering with fear and regret.

"Neither do I. You risked a child's life for money. You would have stood by and let Nick kill Christiana." He turned from her to look into Christiana's bright, honest eyes. Her gentle smile healed the guilt of having brought Kay into the circle of his friends.

Josh looked at the pair, sighing resignedly. Damn Pippa. She had done it again. Now his silver-haired witch would be an automotive bomb waiting to explode.

"I told you so," Pippa murmured wickedly.

Josh pulled his grinning wife into bed, dispensing with the bit of nothing she called a nightgown with the expertise born of long practice. "That has got to be the most aggravating phrase in a wife's vocabulary."

Pippa patted his cheek, giggling. "When are you ordering my Maserati?"

He groaned and flopped back on the pillows, glaring at his spouse, knowing he was beaten but feeling honorbound to at least put up a token fight. "Wouldn't you like a diamond or a trip? Even a boat?"

"I won the bet. The bet was a lavender Maserati. Ergo you owe me my car." She sat Indian-fashion in front of him and folded her arms across her breasts.

His gaze drifted over the picture she made and knew he was lost. "Will you stop posing like a cen-

terfold and at least pretend to have some decorum.''
Even as he objected, his hand trailed over her delicious skin.

She wiggled in delight, but didn't move an inch closer. ''When are you ordering it?''

He sighed. ''Woman, you are one tough lady. I ought to play this game, too.''

She wiggled again, this time with more imagination.

Josh groaned and caved in. ''I ordered it two days ago.''

She threw herself into his arms, laughing. ''I know. And I canceled the order when the man called to check the color.''

He tried to glare but he didn't succeed. ''You witch.''

She kissed him deeply, then raised her head, ignoring the fact that her breath was coming as quickly as his. ''I am the world's worst driver. We both know it. And I want to live to be a really old lady chasing you around the nursing home in my wheelchair.''

He stroked the silver hair falling like pure rain around her face. ''That you can have in lavender, my love,'' he said, relieved that he wouldn't have to worry about her driving. Losing J. Jr. for those hours had only brought home doubly how important his silver-haired siren and their children were to him. He wanted nothing to ever touch them with pain again.

_____ FOURTEEN _____

Christiana slipped out of the shower, feeling the bruises of her ordeal but no longer caring. The euphoria of being back in her room, of knowing that J. Jr. was where he belonged and that Rich had come after her, risking his own life to save her, made the aches and pains of her capture a swiftly fading memory. Walking nude into her bedroom, she stopped short on finding Rich propped up in her bed, the sheets drawn to his bare chest. The soft glow of the lamp on the dressing table spilled gold over him and the room. Their eyes held, his dark with secrets, with knowledge of the future that was yet to be.

He lifted his hand. "Come here." His voice was a husky whisper in the silence. The words of a command, the plea of a man needing his mate.

Her smile was as old as the history of woman as she glided toward him, her body swaying with a grace that would always be hers even with the long passage of years. "You didn't knock."

"Did I need to?" His fingers folded around hers as he looked his fill of her beauty. "We are bound, you and I. I looked into your eyes tonight and saw all my tomorrows."

She touched his face, lightly tracing the strong lines of his features, reading the vulnerability he was no longer making any effort to hide. "And what did you see?"

"A woman capable of laying down her life to save a child. A woman with strength enough to face death and still not lose hope. A woman wise enough to wait for her man to find his own answers."

"Sounds like a paragon. Very uncomfortable people."

He tugged gently on her hand, taking her weight as she came down beside him. "No paragon. My woman has a temper and the strangest shyness about her body. She is stubborn and looks at me as though she can see all the way to my soul." He cupped her face in his hands. "And more than my own life, I love her. I love her smiles, her temper, the slice of her tongue when she is threatened, and her touch. She heals me. She makes me more than I am." He touched his lips to hers, a gentle caress that was all the more powerful for its restraint. "I love you, Christiana. Will you marry me and fill my days with all of you? I promise there will be no shadows from my past to darken our life. I offer you the future for us to paint any way we will."

Tears filled her eyes as she looked back at him. "It took you long enough. I think I've been waiting for you all my life and you've been filling my place with a bunch of witless females that weren't for you."

He laughed at the bite of her words and yanked her against his chest. "Well, damn. Just like a woman. If you hadn't been hiding this gorgeous body in those shrouds you call clothes, I could have found you sooner."

She snuggled into his warmth, holding him tight. "Lecher."

"Lover," he corrected before taking her lips as he would soon claim her body. "Your lover."

"My husband," she murmured, her eyes gleaming with laughter as she had the last word for a long time to come.

SHARE THE FUN . . .
SHARE YOUR NEW-FOUND TREASURE!!

You don't want to let your new books out of your sight?
That's okay. Your friends can get their own. Order below.

No. 7 SILENT ENCHANTMENT by Lacey Dancer
Was she real? She was Alex's true-to-life fairy tale princess.

No. 35 DIAMOND ON ICE by Lacey Dancer
Diana could melt even the coldest of hearts. Jason hasn't a chance.

No. 49 SUNLIGHT ON SHADOWS by Lacey Dancer
Matt and Miranda bring out the sunlight in each other's lives.

No. 59 13 DAYS OF LUCK by Lacey Dancer
Author Pippa Weldon finds her real-life hero in Joshua Luck.

No. 77 FLIGHT OF THE SWAN by Lacey Dancer
Rich had decided to swear off romance for good until Christiana.

No. 1 ALWAYS by Catherine Sellers
A modern day "knight in shining armor." Forever . . . for always!

No. 2 NO HIDING PLACE by Brooke Sinclair
Pretty government agent & handsome professor = mystery & romance.

No. 3 SOUTHERN HOSPITALITY by Sally Falcon
North meets South. War is declared. Both sides win!!!

No. 4 WINTERFIRE by Lois Faye Dyer
Beautiful NY model and rugged Idaho rancher find their own magic.

No. 5 A LITTLE INCONVENIENCE by Judy Christenberry
Liz faces every obstacle Jason throws at her—even his love.

No. 6 CHANGE OF PACE by Sharon Brondos
Can Sam protect himself from Deirdre, the green-eyed temptress?

No. 8 STORM WARNING by Kathryn Brocato
Passion raged out of their control—and there was no warning!

No. 9 PRODIGAL LOVER by Margo Gregg
Bryan is a mystery. Could he be Keely's presumed dead husband?

No. 10 FULL STEAM by Cassie Miles
Jonathan's a dreamer—Darcy is practical. An unlikely combo!

No. 11 BY THE BOOK by Christine Dorsey
Charlotte and Mac give parent-teacher conference a new meaning.

No. 12 BORN TO BE WILD by Kris Cassidy
Jenny shouldn't get close to Garrett. He'll leave too, won't he?

No. 13 SIEGE OF THE HEART by Sheryl McDanel Munson
Nick pursues Court while she wrestles with her heart and mind.

No. 14 TWO FOR ONE by Phyllis Herrmann
What is it about Cal and Elliot that has Leslie seeing double?

No. 15 A MATTER OF TIME by Ann Bullard
Does Josh *really* want Christine or is there something else?

No. 16 FACE TO FACE by Shirley Faye
Christi's definitely not Damon's type. So, what's the attraction?

No. 17 OPENING ACT by Ann Patrick
Big city playwright meets small town sheriff and life heats up.

No. 18 RAINBOW WISHES by Jacqueline Case
Mason is looking for more from life. Evie may be his pot of gold!

No. 19 SUNDAY DRIVER by Valerie Kane
Carrie breaks through all Cam's defenses showing him how to love.

No. 20 CHEATED HEARTS by Karen Lawton Barrett
T.C. and Lucas find their way back into each other's hearts.

Meteor Publishing Corporation
Dept. 292, P. O. Box 41820, Philadelphia, PA 19101-9828

Please send the books I've indicated below. Check or money order only—no cash, stamps or C.O.D.s (PA residents, add 6% sales tax). I am enclosing $2.95 plus 75¢ handling fee for *each* book ordered.

Total Amount Enclosed: $_____.

_____ No. 7	_____ No. 2	_____ No. 9	_____ No. 15
_____ No. 35	_____ No. 3	_____ No. 10	_____ No. 16
_____ No. 49	_____ No. 4	_____ No. 11	_____ No. 17
_____ No. 59	_____ No. 5	_____ No. 12	_____ No. 18
_____ No. 77	_____ No. 6	_____ No. 13	_____ No. 19
_____ No. 1	_____ No. 8	_____ No. 14	_____ No. 20

Please Print:
Name _____
Address _____ Apt. No. _____
City/State _____ Zip _____

Allow four to six weeks for delivery. Quantities limited.